mirage

mirage

Bandula Chandraratna

A PHOENIX HOUSE BOOK
Weidenfeld & Nicolson

First published in Great Britain in 1998
by Serendip Publishers Ltd
This revised edition published in 2000
by Phoenix House

Copyright © Bandula Chandraratna 1998, 2000

The right of Bandula Chandraratna to be identified as the author
of this work has been asserted by him in accordance with the
Copyright, Designs and Patents Act of 1988.

A CIP catalogue record for this book
is available from the British Library.

ISBN 1 861591 84 5

Typeset at The Spartan Press Ltd,
Lymington, Hants
Printed by The Guernsey Press Co. Ltd,
Guernsey, C. I.

Phoenix House

Weidenfeld & Nicolson
The Orion Publishing Group Ltd
Orion House
5 Upper Saint Martin's Lane
London, WC2H 9EA

My parents

The two most wonderful human beings
I have ever known

Chapter 1

It had been a very warm night. Sayeed could not sleep. He lay awake in his hut, which was made up of old wooden boxes gathered from a rubbish dump in the desert. He was wearing his long johns and was soaked with sweat. Through the gaps in the wall and the roof a small breeze blew, cooling the inside of the hut. With it, fine sand from the surrounding desert came in, circulated and settled, on him, on the mattress, and on the few possessions that he had in the one-roomed hut. There were many huts of this type in that area of the desert, and there were hundreds of families living in them. Some families lived in slightly bigger ones, and some of his rich neighbours had more than one hut.

Sayeed lived on his own. He had moved into this hut only two years ago. Before that he had lived in another area of the desert with another group of hut dwellers. That area was too close to the city, and the children who lived there had been hostile to him. So he had moved.

He had only a few essential items in the hut. A single gas burner connected to a propane gas cylinder was sitting on top of a wooden box in a corner. He had a few metal cups and plates in a small cupboard next to the gas ring. In that cupboard he also kept some rice and cans of vegetables and meat, and some spices in glass bottles. He had a small yellow bucket which he used to collect water from the communal water tank. This water was for everything, cooking and washing himself. He also had a plastic jug which he kept for his drinking water. A plastic mat covered the sandy floor, and he slept on a foam mattress with a torn cover. The pillow was a square piece of foam without a case. Originally yellow, the foam pillow had become greyish owing to the accumulation of grease on it. He had a few nails in the wall on which to hang his clothes: two long Arabic *thorbes*, two pairs of long johns and a few pairs of white elasticated shorts which he wore as underwear. He kept some money in a tin box buried in the sand under the mat, but the rest he kept with his friend who was kind to Sayeed, and he trusted him. He had a padlock for the wooden door of the hut, which could be locked only from the outside.

It was quiet. At about three o'clock in the morning, Sayeed got up and went to the cupboard, opened the door and took out the jug of water. He put it to his mouth, drank a few gulps and rubbed his mouth with the back of his hand. After placing the jug back in the cupboard, he went outside. The sky was very dark, except towards the city. Some goats which were sleeping next to his neighbour's hut got up with the opening of the door and made frightened bleats. A light wind started to blow and a few pieces of paper and some plastic bags were swept from the sand and started circling in the air. Sayeed walked barefooted towards the large electricity pylon, along the path which led towards the main road. There was an empty hut near the pylon. Sayeed went behind it and urinated. He kicked some sand to cover the patch of urine and walked back to the hut. He shut the door behind him and lay on the mattress again. He could hear the humming noise of the wind and the sound of sand hitting the wooden huts. He heard a child in a nearby hut wake up and start to cry, followed by the low voice of the mother trying to put him back to sleep. The goats started bleating again and he heard them walk away from the huts. Sayeed was tired now and in a few minutes he was fast asleep.

He was in his early forties, but seemed like a man in his sixties, with his thin frail body and sunken eyes. Sayeed came from a village several hundred kilometres from the city. He owned a small piece of agricultural land there. All his ancestors had been farmers. The only relatives he had left back at the village were his brother's family. His brother had two wives and six children altogether, and they all lived in a mud house in the village. They grew vegetables, and had a few date palm trees, sheep and goats. Sayeed had lived with them before he came to the city looking for work. That was three years ago. His brother had started farming on Sayeed's land and promised to give him his share, which he never did because he was always poor. Both his wives always wanted to buy gold with whatever money he made.

Sayeed brought his savings when he came to the city. He did not know anyone there, and at first he felt very frightened and lonely. So many different kinds of people from different parts of the world were living there. They spoke in different tongues, and some had white skins. That was the first time he saw white people, even though he had heard about them before. Sayeed knew that some of the foreigners belonged to different religions. Their women walked on the street without covering their heads with a veil, and some wore short dresses with short sleeves showing their arms and legs. All this was new to him. The foreigners must be living in sin, he thought.

The most confusing aspect for him was the roads that criss-crossed the city. New roads were laid, new buildings were put up, and the city was expanding constantly, encroaching upon the desert. Trying to cross the road was frightening; the vehicles were driven so fast that almost daily he saw them wrecked.

After a complete day's travel, the driver of the Datsun truck who had brought Sayeed and a few other passengers to the city had dropped them near the bus terminus in the city, collected the fares that they had agreed after haggling, and driven off. Sayeed was lost and did not know where to go. It was getting dark and he was frightened that the police might see him. He had heard about the police, that they could catch anyone wandering in the city, especially at night, and put them in jail. His friends said that the police did this because there were so many foreigners in the city. That night Sayeed slept on a building site. It was dark and quiet there, and he crawled under some scaffolding, cleared the rubble in to a corner, put his head on the bundle of clothes he had brought with him, and went to sleep.

After looking for a job for a few days, he heard about the hospital where they were employing people to work as porters. He put on the clean clothes that he was carrying in his bundle, and went to see the head porter, who was hesitant to employ him because he looked so very thin and weak. But Sayeed said that he drank cardamom coffee every day and that he was as strong as a camel. Then the head porter asked Sayeed to lift a box and carry it from the stores to the main hospital.

Sayeed did this without showing any sign of fatigue. He got the job and was very surprised to hear the high wage he would be getting. It was a lot of money, and he thought that he could buy some camels within a few months, and then he would be rich.

The head porter told him about the shanty town just outside the city, and that he had to spend only a small amount of money to rent a hut, which included the use of the communal water tank. That day after work the head porter took Sayeed to the shanty area which was about five kilometres from the hospital. They found the man who rented these huts, and paid him some money. The head porter took Sayeed to the market to help him buy a mattress, some cooking utensils and a few other essentials. Then he transported them in his car back to Sayeed's new dwelling.

In that hut, Sayeed lived for a year. He disliked the children who used to pester him. The noise of the radios and televisions, and the screaming children got on his nerves. So with the help of one of his friends he built a hut in a new area about fifteen kilometres from the city. It was peaceful when he first moved there two years ago. There had been only a few huts, occupied mainly by elderly people, but during the past year some young families had settled there. Still, this was much better than the old place. He had a few friends in this new neighbourhood, and was sometimes invited for a drink of cardamom coffee.

After about two hours' sleep, Sayeed was woken by the blaring of a loud hailer calling people to prayer. He opened his eyes and looked around the hut. He could see daylight sweeping through the gaps in the wall and the roof. Then he heard the noise of the *mutawah*, the elderly

5

religious leader, yelling, 'Prayer time, prayer time!' and hitting the huts with his cane. The men and the boys started jumping out of their huts, rubbing their eyes and stretching their arms, and they started walking towards the mosque. Just outside the mosque was a big square water tank with six taps fixed to its side. Everyone rushed towards the taps and started washing their ears, eyes, noses and mouths with the running water. Some were gargling, others were blowing their noses and pushing water into their nostrils. They rubbed water on their hair, held their feet under the taps, washed them, and sleepily staggered into the mosque. Sayeed was the last to wash. He straightened his *thorbe*, unfolded the sleeves, put the tooth-brushing stick in his breast pocket, went inside, stood in the back row with his left shoulder almost touching the man next to him, and started praying with the others.

The women were not allowed to pray in the mosque. Some of them prayed in their huts, others slept through the noise of the loud hailer that was fastened to the outside of the mosque.

It was day when they finished praying, and the sky towards the east glowed bright amber.

Sayeed came out of the mosque and started to walk towards his hut. The morning was bright, and cooking smells were coming out of the huts. The goats were wandering among the huts eating thrown-away newspapers and exploring the bits of rubbish. Some were rubbing their bodies against the walls of the huts. There were flies everywhere; the goats were covered with them.

Sayeed did not have a watch. Even if he had had one, he would not have known how to tell the time. Neither could he read. He was surprised when others read the

6

marks that looked like beetles' legs on white paper and said words which they saw written in the paper. Even little children read these scribbles. He could not even tell when the newspapers were the right way up. It all looked the same.

When the sun was just coming over the horizon, it was time to go to the main road and wait for a truck to take him to work. He went back to his hut and took a piece of flat bread and some feta cheese out of the cupboard, opened the bread, put the cheese in it and pressed the bread between his palms, as the cheese squeezed and spread inside. Then he took two olives from a plastic bag and a pickled cucumber from a jar and sucked the vinegar off the outside of the cucumber, put them on the sandwich, rolled it, picked a piece of newspaper from the floor, wiped both sides on his *thorbe*, and wrapped everything with it and put it in his pocket. Then he took a new tooth-brushing stick, put one end in his mouth, wet it and chewed it until some bristles were formed and started cleaning his teeth. He had only a few teeth left, and these were stained dark brown. He pulled his skull cap down, put his white head scarf, the *gutra*, on his head, and threw both hanging ends of it over the top. Then he collected the padlock from the cupboard, went out of the hut, shut the door and locked it and started walking towards the main road.

Two small children were already up and playing in the sand. They wore long dark shirts which came down to their ankles. The smaller one had a runny nose and his eyes were half-closed. Some yellow discharge from his eyes was partially sealing his eyelids together. His hair looked reddish brown, and was covered with dust. The elder boy looked cleaner than the other. He had a toy car in one hand and a can of Pepsi in the other, and was trying to chase the flies away by shaking his head. The small boy had given up chasing the flies, they were on his head, face and body, but he was quite used to them. They both stopped playing when they saw Sayeed coming, and watched him walk on the path. When Sayeed came nearer to them, the smaller boy threw some sand at him, and they both started laughing. Sayeed frowned and pretended to throw an imaginary object at them. But the boys ignored him and started to laugh louder. Sayeed continued walking towards the main road.

Not many vehicles were on the road. A few trucks were going in the opposite direction. Sayeed had to wait for about ten minutes before he managed to stop a truck. It was already half-filled with Yemenis on their way to the city. Sayeed agreed to the fare, climbed over the side of the truck on to its open back, squeezed between two Yemenis and sat down. He raised his head, looked at the faces of his fellow passengers and said, 'Sabaah il-khayr,' and all the passengers replied, 'Sabaah in-nuwr.'

Chapter 2

The truck had stopped on a small road, near the side
entrance to the hospital. Sayeed climbed out, gave the
driver the fare, and walked off. The sun shone over the
hospital buildings. It was beginning to get hot. Sayeed
wiped the sweat off his face with the end of his *gutra*, and
turned in the direction from which the intermittent
sound of a car horn could be heard. A small yellow
Suzuki van which belonged to the post office had slowed
down, and the young driver in it was looking at the
woman who was standing near the gate of the hospital.
She was wearing a black *abaya* which covered her whole
body from head to toe. He pretended to kiss her by
pouting his mouth and smacking his lips. Then he gave
her a passionate smile, accelerated, and drove off.
Sayeed was near the woman and looked at her face,
just visible through the black veil. She appeared very
old, with a wrinkled face covered in sweat, and Sayeed
was angry with the young man who obviously could not
have known whether she was old or young.

People were going to the hospital through the side
gate. Big American cars would stop in the middle of the
road, holding all the other traffic up, and people would
get out, taking their time. All the vehicles behind would
blow their horns, keeping them pressed, and the drivers

would put their heads and hands out of the windows and shout, until the driver got back into his car, shouting back at the other drivers, and drove away.

There were a few street hawkers sitting on the pavement, their backs against the wall, displaying their goods on mats in front of them. They sold cheap toys, children's clothes, and other bric-a-brac from the Far East, always asking a price higher than they wanted, allowing a margin for haggling. Sayeed sat in front of one pavement hawker and started inspecting the wonderful things that were displayed in front of him. Nail clippers with penknives and can openers on them, staplers, scissors, pens, opera glasses, mini accordions, mirrors, make-up, head scarves, handkerchiefs, perfume for men and women, and much more. Sayeed asked the price of a pair of nail clippers, paid slightly less than the man had asked, put them in his pocket, stood up, and walked towards the gate. There was a fat beggar woman leaning quietly against a gate post nearby. Only her outstretched hand was visible, the rest of her was covered completely by the black *abaya*. Sayeed looked at her, but he knew he did not have any coins to give her. He did not want to give her any paper money because he could not afford it. He had seen some people give very generously to beggars, and he thought that these must be rich people.

Some patients were sitting on the dusty clay ground, and children were playing around them. Some were barefooted, covered with dust, and the flies were attracted to them. There were two long queues to get cards for hospital treatment: one queue for men, and the other for women, separated by a metal fence. The office which issued the cards was only a one-roomed small, square, mud-and-brick-built hut, which had two openings in its wall. The two Egyptian clerks sitting behind the Taiwan-made metal office desk were entering the details of patients in their large books and collecting a small fixed charge from everyone. They were taking their time, sipping their hot syrupy tea in small glasses with tiny handles, and smoking their tax-free, king-size American cigarettes, now and then shouting at the nervous patients who had been waiting, queuing for hours in the heat outside. The desert cooler fixed on the wall of the hut kept the temperature inside at a comfortable level, and so the Egyptians were cool.

A few metres to the left of the office stood the mosque, and next to it the staff residential building, a German-built, seven-storey-high block of flats. Doctors, para-medics and some administration staff lived there. The top two floors of this building were occupied by the nurses, who were kept locked in there all the time except when they went to work, and when they were allowed to go shopping. They then wore an *abaya* and a veil over their heads. Not all the nurses were Muslims, but they all had to cover their heads when they went out. The nurses were allowed to go out for two hours a week, including travelling time, escorted by a female warden.

There were a few doctors and nurses coming out of the residential building. The nurses walked directly to the hospital which was about two hundred metres away. The doctors walked to the administration building to sign their names in the register.

The hospital building was very old. It had only an eighty-bed capacity. Behind it stood the concrete skeleton of the new hospital which was to have replaced it. The American company contracted to build it had gone bankrupt, so the four-storey huge concrete structure which was to have provided a three-hundred-bed-capacity hospital looked like a building in Hiroshima after the bomb had been dropped.

A few metres from the hospital stood the pre-fabricated, two-storey building which had the hospital laboratory on the ground floor, and the administration offices and the hospital director's office on the first. A wooden staircase fixed to the outside of the building was the only access to the first floor. Next to this building stood the pharmacy which had two holes in the wall: one for male patients, the other for female. It was entirely staffed by Egyptians. The hospital drivers' room was next to it. This had a metal bed with a foam mattress and dirty blanket on it. In the corner of this room, next to the desert cooler, stood the refrigerator, and on top of this was a small Japanese black-and-white television set. All the drivers were Egyptian and they all spoke in very loud voices.

Sayeed walked towards the administration building, climbed the wooden stairs and went into the office where they left the attendance register. There were two registers: one for the foreign workers and another for the locals. The Egyptian clerk gave Sayeed a pad of ink and showed him where his name was on the register. Sayeed pressed his thumb on the pad, pressed it again in front of his name, and rubbed his thumb and forefinger together. Then he adjusted his *gutra* and went out of the room. He went down the steps and through the doorway under the stairs to the laboratory where he worked. He went into the sitting-room. His friend Hameed was having his breakfast.

Hameed was a young Yemeni in his early twenties

who also worked as a porter. He shared a flat with some Pakistani workers in the overcrowded area of the city where underpaid migrant labourers lived. Most of the time, he stayed in the laboratory and slept either in an armchair or on a white hospital sheet on the floor of the microbiology media pouring room. He got his meals free from the hospital kitchen, did his washing in the laboratory, and hung everything, including his underwear, on a line in a corner of the biochemistry department.

'Salaam alaykum, Hameed,' Sayeed said.

'Wa-alaykum is-salaam,' Hameed replied.

Hameed asked Sayeed to join him for breakfast, which he had brought from the hospital kitchen. It was boiled eggs with peta bread and olives, and pieces of feta cheese. Hameed was pouring some oily mixture which he had brought from Yemen on the bread to soften it and to give it more flavour. The mixture was in an empty Shelltox insect killer can, whose spray nozzle had been removed and replaced with a sealed lead top with holes in it. Sayeed said that he had brought something with him and thanked Hameed for his offer. Sayeed took his bread out of his pocket and put it on the table. Hameed started to feed his parrot which was in its cage on the table. He had caught this parrot when it was perching on a palm tree in the hospital grounds, and had bought a cage for it and kept it in the laboratory sitting-room. There were objections from the others, but he ignored them. He was getting very attached to it, and was trying to teach it to speak.

Sayeed shook the electric kettle to see whether it had any water in it, and found there was just enough for one cup. He plugged the kettle in and tilted it backwards to allow the small amount of water to touch the filament, and held it until the steam came out through the lid. He poured the water into a glass, and put two tea bags and a few spoons of sugar in it. He put the kettle, which gave off a burning smell, on the table, and stirred the tea with a wooden spatula, shaking the tea bags up and down in the glass with the other hand. Then he threw the tea bags in the bin, took his cup of tea and went to sit next to Hameed at the table, with the parrot cage in front of him.

It was almost half past seven, and the patients were waiting at reception, either to have their blood tests or to collect their laboratory reports. The receptionist and the male phlebotomist, both Egyptians, came on duty but went to the sitting-room directly to have their breakfast. Magidi, the receptionist, who was a very fat person, sat down in the sitting-room with a large tub of plain yoghurt and a small tin of Kraft cheese, and some peta bread, and a pint bottle of sterilised milk. He took out his Swiss army penknife, opened the tin of cheese, ate the lump in one mouthful, and started eating the yoghurt with the small spoon of his penknife. He took large bites off the flat peta bread, washing everything down with the pint of sterilised milk. The phlebotomist, Salim, filled the kettle with water, plugged it in, and put a tea bag in a glass. He put his hand in the sugar tin, took out a handful of sugar, filled about one third of the glass with it, and when the water started boiling, poured it into the glass, and stirred it with a wooden spatula. He dropped the tea bag on the table, lit a king-size Marlboro, sat down in one of the armchairs, started drinking the tea with a sucking noise, and smoked the cigarette.

'Lot of patients out there today,' Salim said.

'Yes, I know. It gives me a headache when they all start shouting at the same time,' Magidi replied.

'I must have a smoke and relax before all that,' said Salim.

'They use very bad language. Most of them are Bedouins,' Magidi said.

'Some of them are very smelly. Straight from the desert, and probably never had a bath in their lives,' Salim added, and he laughed loudly.

'Don't speak so loud. If a local hears we will all be in trouble,' Magidi warned.

'Well, Sayeed is here, he's a local.' Salim laughed again with his shoulders shaking.

'Sayeed is different. He's a nice person, and he doesn't talk much anyway. Isn't that right?' asked Magidi.

Sayeed smiled and nodded.

Nura, the Egyptian phlebotomist, came into the sitting-room.

'Sabaah il-khayr,' she said, chewing gum with her mouth opening wide.

'Sabaah in-nyur,' everyone replied.

Nura made herself a glass of tea, and sat down comfortably in a large armchair. Just then, a female patient in a black *abaya* walked into the sitting-room.

'Aren't you going to do any work?' she shouted. 'We have been waiting for hours, while you people just sit here drinking tea!'

'You are not supposed to be here. Go to the women's sitting-room,' said Magidi.

'I will not move from here until someone comes to see us. You foreigners are all the same. I pray to God to send you back to your countries, where you will be without work, begging on the street.' Everyone smiled, but did not turn round.

'So, are you going to do your work or not?' the woman asked.

'Go back to reception, we will be there soon,' Magidi said in a loud angry voice.

The woman started swearing and walked back to reception. Salim and Nura slowly got up, and went to the bleeding rooms, with Magidi following. Hameed was laughing loudly, but Sayeed was sitting with a frightened look on his face.

'I hope my parrot doesn't pick up her language,' Hameed said.

Sayeed was quiet, picked up a newspaper and started reading.

'Sayeed, that is upside down,' Hameed said, and Sayeed turned the newspaper the right way up, and pretended he was reading. Then Mohammad Rafi, the chief technician in the laboratory, walked in sleepily.

'Where is everyone?' Mohammad asked.

'The Biochemistry technicians are late today,' Hameed replied.

'What about Microbiology and Haematology?' Mohammad asked.

'Well, some are already working in Microbiology, but the Haematology people are late today,' Hameed said.

'If they are fifteen minutes late, Administration will take the register away. Then they will lose a day's pay,' Mohammad said.

'Is this a new rule?' Hameed asked.

'Yes,' replied Mohammad.

At that point, the Scottish technicians walked in, talking among themselves as they came. George Fielding with his wife, Pamela; Jim MacMurray; Ian Paton with his wife, Margaret. They all lived in the hospital residents' building.

'Morning, Mohammad,' said George.

'You are late today!' Mohammad warned.

'I'm sorry. I didn't wake up,' George said.

'Late-night party, was it?' Mohammad grinned.

'Well, I have a slight headache,' George replied, and he walked with his wife to the biochemistry department where they worked. The rest went to the microbiology section.

Abdul Mubarak, the local technician who worked in Biochemistry, walked into the sitting-room and asked Sayeed to bring him a liver sandwich from the cafeteria near the airport road. Sayeed agreed, and Abdul Mubarak took some money out of the breast pocket of his *thorbe*, held it a few centimetres away from his bulging eyes, checked it well, and gave some to Sayeed. Mohammad was watching this and seemed annoyed.

'This is not the time to eat. You should be working now,' he said.

Abdul Mubarak got angry. His myopic eyes seemed to bulge even more as he told Mohammad that he could not work on an empty stomach. Mohammad did not want to argue with him, because even though he was the chief technician, he was still a foreigner. The locals, though juniors, disliked taking orders from foreigners, since they considered themselves superior to everyone else. Abdul Mubarak, who fought, argued with and upset everyone in the laboratory, was not a person to confront. Mohammad did not say anything else, and Abdul Mubarak went into the biochemistry department. Sayeed stood there for a while watching Abdul and

Mohammad, then adjusted his *gutra*, and went out to get the camel-liver sandwich.

Mohammad took out a dry cheese roll from his pocket, and started to eat it with very little appetite. He had had surgery on a gastric ulcer some time ago, so he ate little but frequently, and that very reluctantly. George Fielding and his colleague Nimal came from Biochemistry, and sat next to Mohammad.

'Haven't you got any work to do?' Mohammad asked.

'We want to ask you something, Mohammad,' said George.

'What?'

'We collected our overtime yesterday and it seems very little. I was on call for about ten days last month, plus one weekend, but the money I got paid is very little,' George said.

'I will calculate it again, and if it should be different, we will tell Administration,' Mohammad said.

'How do you calculate it?' George asked.

'It is very complicated. You know that they do not pay for the first fifteen hours you are on call, don't you?' Mohammad said.

'Yes, yes, that is what it says in the contract, even though I think it is unfair, and I heard the locals get paid for all the on-call hours,' George said.

'That is not your business, is it?' Mohammad replied.

Nimal had a similar complaint, and Mohammad told both of them he would look into the problem. Then Abdul Mubarak walked in and started to shout at George and Nimal, saying that they were all busy in the laboratory, and there was no time to sit around.

'It's high time you did some bloody work as well,' George said to Abdul.

'I am going to complain to the director of the hospital about you,' Abdul said.

'You just do that,' said George, and he was getting up to go back to the biochemistry section when Ian Paton walked in to ask Mohammad for the storeroom key because he wanted some Petri dishes.

Mohammad took the key out of his pocket and gave it to Ian. He looked at George, and asked him whether he needed anything from the stores. George said he needed some reagents for one of his machines, and that he would come with Ian, and he asked Nimal to come as well to carry some of it back. Abdul had by this time calmed down slightly, and went back to his section, still threatening to complain.

'That guy is crazy,' George said.

'Yes, we know that, but don't argue with him. He's like a mad dog. He will keep on jumping at you if you annoy him,' Mohammad warned.

'You don't have to annoy him. He picks on everyone, and we have to watch every word we say. He can't see very well, but his hearing is very sharp. Even if you whisper something at the end of the room, he can hear you. The other day someone mentioned the word beer, and he threatened to go to the religious police.'

'That must have been you, Nimal,' Mohammad replied.

'I meant non-alcoholic beer. There is plenty of that here. What is wrong in saying the word beer? Alcohol is banned, but plenty of home-made stuff is drunk here. Perhaps he does not know that,' Nimal said.

'My goodness. You don't seem to realise that some of these people are very religious. These are very sensitive things. Anything connected with religion is sensitive.

Please be careful. If he complains to the religious police, they will throw you in jail, or deport you. These people lie so much, they could even say you brew beer, then what would happen? They would come and search your house,' Mohammad said.

Nimal looked very worried, and did not say anything. George smiled at him.

'Let's go, boys,' Ian said, and he walked out of the sitting-room. George and Nimal followed him.

Ian collected a trolley from the preparatory room, and pushed it towards the door, as Sayeed came through with the sandwich for Abdul.

'Kayf haalak, Sayeed?' Ian asked.

'Al-hamdulillah. Shukran,' replied Sayeed.

Ian asked Arafat, one of the other technicians, to ask Sayeed in Arabic to come to the storeroom with him because there were a few things to bring. Arafat, a Palestinian refugee from Jordan who had worked as a junior technician, spoke to Sayeed, and Sayeed nodded his head in agreement, and said he would give the sandwich to Abdul and come to the stores. Ian thanked him, and pushed the trolley out through the side door.

'I hope the wee bugger doesn't change his mind,' Ian muttered.

George laughed, put his hand on the trolley, and helped Ian to push it towards the staff residential building, where one of the ground-floor flats was used as a storeroom.

'I'm fed up with this bloody dump,' George said, adjusting his darkening spectacles.

'Well, son, you know what they say. Take it or leave it!' Ian said.

'I would like to leave tomorrow. No, today if possible. But the bastards won't give me my passport, or the exit visa, until I finish my contract. You know that! That means another seven months in this burning hell-hole,' George said.

'You could always break your contract and go. It might mean paying money to them, and buying your own air ticket back. I know living here is difficult. But it's worth putting up with the inconvenience. The money they pay here is twice as much as in England. Sorry! In the United Kingdom, I mean,' Nimal said.

'They can shove their money up their . . .' George started, but Ian stopped him and pointed to a little boy urinating on to the base of a date palm tree.

The hospital garden, which spread from the residential building to the laboratory, had a few date palms and some flowering shrubs. Visitors and patients would sit there with their families, drinking tea which they had brought with them from home, in large Chinese-made vacuum flasks, while their children played on the grass patch. Some children would tread on cannas and other flowering plants, others would tear the petals and leaves off them. The visitors were either waiting to see relatives, or waiting till the clinics opened to get some treatment for themselves. In the middle of the park was the manhole cover of the big sewage pit. All the sewage from the hospital emptied into it. When it was full, a Mercedes tanker would come and pump up the sewage and take it to the sterile desert and empty it out. The whole area around the hospital would stink for a few days, but after a day or two people would begin to get used to it, though never completely.

Ian and George wheeled the trolley to the ground floor of the residential block. They had flats on the ground floor, a few doors away from the storeroom. Whenever they needed replacements for their broken lamp fittings or shower hoses, this storeroom provided the spares. If they had asked Administration for replacements, they would have had to pay for the damage, which would have involved seeing the people in Administration several times on different days, and writing letters. So it was much easier and more peaceful to take the spares from the storeroom secretly and replace them with the broken ones.

As they went inside, Sayeed appeared from somewhere and followed them. Ian picked up a two-and-a-half-litre bottle of pure alcohol and gave George a smile.

'You aren't! Are you?' George asked him.

'Yes I am, son,' Ian said, and placed the bottle on the bottom shelf of the trolley.

'Sayeed is here. What are you going to do about him?' Nimal asked.

'Nay problem, son. Just you watch,' Ian said, and he picked up a bottle of hydrochloric acid, and a box of sensitivity discs, and gave them to Sayeed.

'Off you go, shagger!' Ian said to Sayeed.

Sayeed gave a smile, put the box on one of his shoulders, and, with the acid bottle pressed against his chest, walked away.

'Now, son, put the box of Petri dishes on the top of the trolley, and a few bits and pieces in the bottom section, and we will go past my flat on our way out,' Ian said with a smile.

They loaded the trolley, pushed it outside, shut the door, and looked to see whether anyone was about, and when they found that everything was clear, wheeled the trolley into Ian's flat. Ian took the bottle of pure alcohol and hid it in the wardrobe behind his wife's dresses, and pushed the trolley back into the corridor.

'Leave the trolley over there for a wee while, and come into the kitchen,' Ian said.

In the kitchen, Ian took a bottle of grape juice from behind the refrigerator, and poured some dark frothy liquid into three glasses.

'What is it?' Nimal asked.

'Taste it and see,' Ian replied.

Nimal tasted it and asked whether it was wine.

'Beer,' Ian said.

'So, you went to the supermarket? I told you which supermarket was selling malt extract,' Nimal said.

George and Ian laughed and drank their cloudy dark brown beer, which did not taste anything like normal beer.

'I don't think they know what malt extract is used for,' Nimal said.

'I can't think of any other use for it,' said George.

'They put tins of yeast next to it,' Ian said, and all three laughed.

'Must be the Americans. They must have convinced the locals that it's used for making bread or something,' George said.

'It's not quite ready yet, that's why it is cloudy, but I couldn't wait another week, so I bottled it up,' Ian said, lighting a cigarette.

Nimal felt tipsy, since this was the first alcoholic drink he had tasted for about six months, but he felt happy.

'That bottle of pure alcohol is for the party. I'm going to make a lovely punch with it,' Ian said.

'You know, if we get caught the bastards can flog us publicly. Eighty lashes they say, and about three years in one of their hellish jails,' Nimal said.

'Now, now, don't worry, son. Who's going to suspect us, umm? Just don't worry,' Ian said.

'Bastards raided the British Aircraft Corporation compound and took some poor guys to jail. Apparently they were distilling grappo and sadeki,' George said.

'I suppose the company will get them out. The only thing is that they will lose their jobs, and get deported straightaway,' Nimal said.

'They must be wondering what happened to us,' said Ian. 'Have a puff of smoke to get the smell of beer off your breath,' he suggested.

'I've got some chewing gum,' Nimal said.

'It might not be enough,' Ian warned.

Nimal and George borrowed Ian's cigarette, but smoked only a few puffs, as they usually did not smoke.

After the midday prayer Sayeed sat in the sitting-room, having joined Hameed for lunch, which the hospital provided free to porters, and which Hameed had brought from the kitchen in two Chinese-made stacking containers. There was boiled rice, boiled goat's meat, some highly viscous and slimy dark green spinach soup, and some peta bread. Hameed put his mouth to the soup dish, ate all of it, along with some rice and meat, smacking his lips. Sayeed soaked his bread in the soup, then ate it with some difficulty with the few teeth he had left. The tough goat meat was difficult to eat, and Sayeed struggled to tear small shreds from the chunk with his wobbly teeth, carefully separating small pieces of bone from it. After they had had enough of this, they ate an apple each, and drank a small can of syrupy mango juice. Hameed started clearing the table, and Sayeed went to an armchair in a corner, sat down, put his legs up, rested his head on the back of the chair, and closed his eyes. He went to sleep in no time, and no one disturbed him. He had a habit of sleeping after lunch every day. He could go to sleep soundly even when the Egyptians were talking.

The loud hailer from the hospital mosque started broadcasting the afternoon prayer call, and Abdul came rushing into the sitting-room, shook Sayeed awake, and told him it was *salaa* time. Sayeed lifted his head and wiped the trickle of sputum from the side of his mouth with his *gutra*, put his legs down, looked around with red eyes, got up and walked towards the toilet on wobbly legs, swaying slightly, to have his prayer wash. He took his *gutra* off, hung it on the handle of the toilet door which he left open, and took his toothbrush stick, rubbed it on his teeth a few times, gargled loudly and spat in the sink, then put the stick back in his breast pocket. Then he blew his nose with his fingers, and held them under running water, rinsed them, and took handfuls of water and washed his nose, ears, eyes, touched his hair with his wet hand, rubbing water on it. Then he put one foot at a time into the sink and washed it, shook the water off, and put his dusty leather sandals back on, wiped his hands on his *thorbe*, wiped his face with the *gutra* and put it back on his head, and finally walked towards the mosque.

Men were already walking in. Sayeed left his slippers near the entrance.

After the prayer, Sayeed went back to the laboratory and had some tea. That afternoon he had to help Mohammad bring some new furniture from the main hospital stores.

When it reached five in the afternoon, everyone rushed upstairs to sign out, before going home.

Sayeed came out of the hospital grounds. The airport road was busy, and traffic jams were beginning to build up. The sun was going down, but it was still very hot. Sayeed walked towards the main bus station to get some transport home. It was about two kilometres to the bus stop from the hospital, and Sayeed enjoyed walking. He could look at the big houses with tall walls around them. He had heard that very rich people lived in those houses with many servants and several cars. He had heard that these houses had big swimming pools, and he had even heard that their women swam in them too. Sayeed used to swim in the small stream that flowed near his village, when he was a child, a long time ago. He had very pleasant memories of that. Some of the big houses had armed guards in uniform, sitting near the gate. Sayeed thought very important rich people must live in those houses. Some day he expected to be rich as well, and live in a big house, with one or two beautiful wives, and then he too could give paper money to the beggars.

Chapter 3

The heat was intense. Palm trees, their leaves covered with a thin layer of dust, stood still. The red and orange cannas had torn petals and leaves, and dust marks in the shape of water drops from the morning watering. The dry scanty grass on the red clay of the square where the palm trees stood scorched in the blazing sun.

The clay-coloured derelict-looking old hospital building stood a few yards from this green patch, and a dried-out and broken water fountain stood next to the green patch, in front of the hospital. The residential block stood to the right of the main hospital, and the building with the administration offices and the laboratory stood to the left. The grounds were spacious, and covered with light brown hard clay.

The temperature during midsummer could go above one hundred and thirty degrees Fahrenheit. In the middle of the desert where the city was, the humidity was very low; it was dry heat. Very few people worked outside at midday in midsummer because they would lose large amounts of body water and rapidly become dehydrated. People like the manual labourers who worked for construction companies, building roads, or who did other construction work, had to labour outside, and they consumed large amounts of water for their constant thirst.

Only a few vehicles could be seen on the roads. Most shops were closed at midday, and opened again in the evening when the air was cool. Afternoon was siesta time. The employees of the hospital who worked on the double shift, a morning shift and an evening shift, went home during the afternoon, and after their meal, some of them went to sleep. Because the evenings were cooler, the hospital was open for outpatient clinics and other treatment till about nine in the evening, and those who worked on a single day shift had long tea breaks, sitting in air-conditioned rooms. Some went to sleep in their chairs.

Sayeed was sitting in one of the Taiwan-made brown-vinyl-covered easy chairs, in the sitting-room, with his head resting on one of the one-inch-thick, square-shaped, chrome-plated arm rests, his feet resting on another chair, and his head scarf, the gutra, covering his eyes to hide the glare of the bright fluorescent light. His mouth was slightly open, he was breathing through it, and was fast asleep. Next to him Hameed was sleeping in another chair. No one else was in the sitting-room. It was quiet. Now and then footsteps came from the bio-chemistry section next door. On the side of the sitting-room a clear glass partition separated the sitting-room from the biochemistry section, and on the opposite side was a similar partition; the haematology section was on the other side. Now and then the silence was broken when a centrifuge started in the biochemistry section, or by the noise of running water, or the tapping noise that came from the pipetting of blood samples to the Beckmann analyser machines, or from someone clearing their throat, and spitting in a sink or paper bin. The constant blowing noise that came from the air-conditioners was something you got used to. It kept the inside air cool and humid.

Dr Fatima, the haematologist, was sitting at her desk in a corner in the small haematology section, about two feet away from the ladies' toilet. She was reading a book, and a pile of forms was waiting for her signature in a wire basket on her desk. Ismail, the haematology technician, was looking down a microscope, and counting a blood film.

James Logan, the biochemistry technician, picked up a metal bucket, used to collect broken glass, which was kept under the bench where the Beckman enzyme analyser was; he slowly tiptoed into the sitting-room, placed it next to Sayeed's chair, and went back to the biochemistry section, picked up an empty 7Up can, aimed well, and threw it into the bucket. It made a loud noise, and Sayeed and Hameed both woke up. Sayeed removed the head scarf from his face, sat up in his chair, and looked around to see what had happened. Hameed stood up suddenly, and started swearing at the person who made the noise; but they did not know who threw the can. Abdul Mubarak came shouting in, pulling James by his hand.

'He is mad!' Abdul said.

'Why do you want to disturb that poor man? What has he done to you?' he asked.

'Sorry, Sayeed,' said James, picking up the bucket, and he went back to the biochemistry section. Sayeed gave a big smile, showing the few teeth he had left. Then he stretched his right hand, and with his palm open he stiffly moved his hand upwards, and jerked his head

29

backwards, gesticulating 'What's the matter with you?' which everyone understood. There was no anger in Sayeed; no one had ever seen anger in him.

Sayeed got up, switched the kettle on, and asked Hameed whether he would like some tea as well; but he sat there, still angry, and refused.

'I am going to see my family next weekend,' Sayeed said.

'Are you really, Sayeed?' Hameed asked.

'Yes, it has been a long time.'

'Isn't it very far away?'

'It takes more than half a day to get there.'

'Your brother lives there, doesn't he?' Hameed asked.

'Yes, my brother and his wives and their children live there. Some of that land belongs to me, and my brother farms on that,' Sayeed said.

'Do they give you any money for that?' Hameed asked.

'No, no, he is my brother. How can I take any money from him?'

'Does he do any other work except farming?' Hameed asked.

'No. What else can you do in a village? He grows a few vegetables. He also has some goats and chickens.'

'How many children has he got?'

'I don't know really. All I know is that he has many girls, and only a few boys,' Sayeed replied.

'He must have been quite busy,' Hameed said with a smile on his face.

Sayeed switched off the steaming kettle, and poured a glass of tea for himself.

'Why did you kill the cat, Hameed?' Sayeed asked,

and put the hot glass of tea on the table in the middle of the room, and sat by it.

'He killed my parrot,' Hameed said.

'How did he do it? He was in the cage, wasn't he?' Sayeed asked.

'He opened the cage and ate the parrot,' Hameed said.

'That was very bad,' said Nabeil, one of the porters, who heard the conversation as he walked into the sitting-room.

'I got a broom, cornered him in that part of the sitting-room, pushed the broom at his throat, pressed him against the wall and held the broom there until he went limp. He was struggling and making noises,' Hameed said, and gave a big laugh.

'I don't think that was necessary,' Sayeed said.

'My poor parrot. I spent money and bought that cage, and he was beginning to talk,' Hameed said, pointing to the empty bird cage which was on top of the filing cabinet.

Nabeil, who was new to the place, did not want to say anything, but he shook his head in disbelief.

Salim, the Sudanese technician who worked in the biochemistry section, came into the sitting-room, sat next to Nabeil, and asked him for a cigarette. Nabeil put his hand in the side pocket of his long Arabic dress, took out a packet of Rothmans cigarettes, and a lighter; he opened the packet, took one cigarette out, and gave it to Salim. He took another one, put it in his mouth, lit it with the lighter, and held the flame for Salim. Then he sucked a long breath of smoke, held it there for a while, and let it out slowly through his nostrils.

'Sukran,' Salim said.

Nabeil tilted his head to one side, and gave him a smile, put the index finger of his left hand in his mouth, and started rubbing his finger on his front teeth.

'How do you like the work?' Salim asked.

'Well, it is all right. There is not much to do,' Nabeil replied.

'Abdul Mubarak wants me to sit in a chair in the biochemistry room, because I am the porter especially for that section. So, he is going to find a chair,' Nabeil said.

'I guess, then, Sayeed is for Haematology, and Microbiology, and you are going to be only for our section. That is good. But, apart from bringing things from the stores, and bringing sandwiches, and Pepsi from the shops, there is not much work to do,' Salim said with a smile.

Sayeed sat at the table drinking his tea. He was sucking it through a small gap in his tight lips, with a stream of air, so it was not too hot on his tongue. Very hot and strong plain tea refreshed Sayeed. He tried to recall the tea that he used to drink back in his village. His brother's first wife used to put crushed cardamoms in tea; drinking that, sitting outside the house on a cool evening, was heavenly, Sayeed thought. Mohammad Zain, the Sudanese haematology technician, added a stick of cinnamon to tea. Sayeed had never tasted that. He thought, perhaps one day, he would try cinnamon tea as well. He watched the foreigners who worked in the laboratory adding milk to their tea. He could not imagine how anyone could drink it like that.

Salim and Nabeil were sitting quietly, smoking their cigarettes. Hameed was turning the pages of a magazine.

Then they heard the loud hailer with a prayer call, and it was prayer time again.

Abdul Mubarak came and tapped on the glass partition and said: 'Salah, salah.' Everyone slowly got up, and walked towards the toilet to have their wash before the prayer.

Chapter 4

It was about eight o'clock in the morning. The sun was shining above the clay-coloured hotel building which stood next to the bus terminal where Datsun and Toyota minibuses with their embellished roof racks were parked, cassette players and radios blaring out Arabic music. The drivers were calling out for passengers, yelling where they would be going, and how much the fares were. The passengers were piling on to the buses with their cases, and securing them with nylon ropes, so that they would not get thrown away as the vehicles were driven at great speed on desert tracks, falling in pot holes, throwing the passengers into the air, their heads almost touching the roof. As they swayed from side to side, pushing each other by their shoulders, the passengers would press their feet hard on the floor to keep their balance, still looking out through the thick cloud of dust the vehicle was making, to enjoy the scenery. The bus terminal, which was on empty land in the busiest area of the city, was not purpose-built. Its uneven ground was covered with light brown clay, hardened owing to vehicles constantly driving over it, and as a result the parked minibuses tilted to one side. The buses were always parked facing the small tarred road which ran from the city centre through this area towards the east of the city. On the other side of the road a huge ditch about five metres wide had been dug up for the burial of a sewage pipe to collect waste from all the dwellings around that area, and pump it to the middle of the desert a few kilometres away. Facing the road from the bus stand was the canvas *souk* where they made tents and covers for vehicles. Behind the bus stand stood the smoke-house where people went for a relaxing smoke, lying or sitting on high couches and sipping hot glasses of sweet plain tea. Unprocessed tobacco leaves were crushed and positioned on the pipe, with some red-hot charcoal placed over it. The smoke was sucked through the water at the bottom of the pipe, making a noise like a drainpipe being unblocked. This needed strong lung power, because of the large column of air that had to be sucked. Only a small amount of smoke came out of the sucking end. Most of it was lost at the burning end.

Opposite the canvas *souk*, on the other side of the bus stand, stood a hotel where the newly arrived guest workers got a bed for the night. Large green desert coolers were fixed on the outside of each room. The ground floor of the hotel had been converted into shops which sold electrical goods, ranging from televisions to washing machines. Next to the hotel was a row of shops selling everything from food to stationery. There was a shop selling fruit juice in this row. They sold crushed and squeezed fruit juices, undiluted, in plastic cups over the counter. Oranges, lemons, bananas, apples, cane sugar stems, papayas, mangoes, and even carrots were used for crushing to juice.

Sayeed came to this bustling, noisy bus terminal wearing his cleanest *thorbe* and with a bundle containing some of his clothes and some presents for his brother's family. The terminal was crowded with men. No women were allowed on these buses. Sayeed had to walk between the closely parked minibuses until he found the one which would take him to his village. Sayeed haggled over the price, and climbed into the bus, looking for a window seat near the middle. He knew a rear seat would be too bumpy on a long ride. Sayeed pushed his bundle under a seat and sat down. There were a few people already sitting.

Sayeed wiped his face with one end of his *gutra*, and blew his nose and wiped it using the other end. It was beginning to get hot. Now and then a thick cloud of dust would rise when a moving vehicle passed on the dust-covered edges of the tarred road which ran in front of the stand, and Sayeed would hold his breath as long as he could. Then he would hold the edge of the *gutra* over his nostrils, breathing slowly until the dust cloud became thin and dispersed. His eyes were beginning to get sore. He looked around the bus, and saw a few people trying to sleep. He placed his head on the side, slid down a little in his seat, closed his eyes, and tried to sleep too.

He could not. His mind was restless. He thought of his brother's family back at the village, and of the welcome that he might get. He thought of the people at work, Hameed's parrot, and the cat he had killed. He thought of Abdul Mubarak, and his arrogance, and he thought of the cool, air-conditioned sitting-room where everyone sat and drank their tea and went to sleep in their chairs. He thought of his hut in the city. He hoped that no one would damage his hut, or steal anything from it. He did not like the mischievous little children who lived around there.

He felt very thirsty, and could not keep his eyes closed any longer. He got up, took out his bundle and put it on his seat, asked the man sitting behind him to keep an eye on his place, got off the bus, and went towards the little girl who was selling soft drinks. She was about eight years old, and was crouching with her crumpled red dress with large yellow flowers tucked between her legs, leaning against a lamppost. Her uncombed hair was brown, her black face had dust marks on it, and her black ankles and feet were covered with layers of dust. Her sad, small eyes with a yellowish discharge still attached to their lids were partially open, and her constantly runny nose, which she kept wiping with the back of her hand, reminded Sayeed of children back at his village. She had a large blue plastic basin in front of her. There were a few blocks of ice in it, in a pool of black water. Among these a few cans of 7Up and Pepsi were wedged. Whenever she sold a can, she would take another from the crates on either side of her and put it in the basin to cool. Sayeed bought two cans each of 7Up and Pepsi. He put two in his right pocket, and another in the left, and kept a can of 7Up in his hand. As he walked towards the bus, he wiped the edge of the can which he would put in his mouth with the end of his *thorbe* sleeve, opened it and flicked the metal ring to the ground, pouring a large mouthful into his mouth. He swirled it around, enjoying the sweet metallic taste of the drink, and the coolness of the gaseous mixture inside his mouth. He swallowed small amounts slowly, and his throat got cooler, his body became refreshed, and his thirst was slowly quenched. Sayeed gulped a few more mouthfuls while standing just outside the entrance to the bus, and the gas inside the drink made his eyes tearful. It was hot outside, so he went inside the bus, put his bundle under the seat, and sat down. The bus was beginning to fill up. Sayeed wiped his eyes with the cool water from the outside of the can, placed the can over his right cheek, and started rolling it backwards and forwards on his cheek. A few people were fanning themselves with newspapers or magazines, but Sayeed had nothing to fan himself with.

The driver climbed on to the bus, collected the money from the passengers and sat in his seat. He arranged the mirror so that he could see himself in it, adjusted his *gutra*, rubbed his moustache with the fingertips of both hands, and rubbed and pulled his beard with his right hand. He opened his lips to check his teeth, took a toothbrush stick out of his breast pocket, chewed the end to a pulp, and started brushing his brown teeth. He adjusted the mirror again so that he could see through the back window of the minibus. Then he checked whether anyone else was getting on. When he discovered no one, he asked one of the passengers to close the folding door, and started the bus. The radio began blaring at the same time.

The bus moved forward slowly, rocking from side to side as it went over the hardened clay bumps on the bus stand. Sayeed tried to steady himself by holding on to the top end of the seat in front of him, and all the passengers swayed as the bus moved. It came to the tarred road, turned left and drove towards the east of the city through the crowded market area. Almost all the shops were open. The hawkers were getting their mats laid on the pavement and their goods placed on them. After the busy market they came to a quieter quarter where brown blocks of flats were built. The roads were wider here. Now and then they would pass a dust-covered palm tree with dry torn leaves. When they came to the outskirts of the city, the road ran by the large carpet *souk*, where they sold carpets of all types. Some carpets were hanging over tall beams that were tied to palm trees, and some were rolled up or piled into heaps, or laid over the roofs of trucks. Most of these carpets were very expensive. Sayeed heard that some of them came from other countries, and he also knew that he would never be able to afford one. In his brother's house they had a beautiful red carpet which his brother had to buy when he got married a few years ago. His sister-in-law would hang it outside and hit it with a stick to get rid of the dust.

The road was getting narrower and pot holes appeared more frequently. The driver tried to avoid them, but occasionally they were so close to each other that the wheels would go in, throwing the passengers up and down.

Finally they came to the beginning of the stretch of road that would take them to Sayeed's village. The road was narrow, just wide enough for two vehicles to pass. Near the kerb the tarred surface was broken where heavy vehicles had been driven at high speed too near the edge.

It was getting hotter, and the windows of the minibus were kept shut because the outside air blasting through the open windows was very hot, and when it hit your face, it was like opening an oven door. In the middle of the desert the air was very dry, and people would sweat. The sweat evaporated quickly, and kept everyone cool. But it was this constant sweating and the loss of salt which made people thirsty and lethargic.

Now and then a vehicle travelling in the other direction would pass, causing a sudden gust of wind. Someone overtaking would press their horn, and sometimes keep it pressed while they passed the minibus at great speed, throwing up dust clouds. The whole length of the road was in a state of rising and settling clouds of dust. They had been travelling for about half an hour, and were about twenty-five kilometres from the city. This was the only road all the way to the horizon. There was no sign of any house or tree to be seen. The light brown undulating desert, scattered with rough brown rocks and scanty sun-scorched bushes, stretched all around as far as the eye could see.

Not many vehicles were travelling on this stretch of road. The passengers were dozing off to sleep, the bus travelling at a steady speed. The driver had turned off the radio. Only the engine noise, and the rumbling of the tyres, broke the silence.

Sometimes, small dried-up bushes would roll away, bumping and flying like balls in the desert. Mini tornadoes would form, and suck up dust and old plastic bags, papers and broken pieces of twig, and take them high up in the sky, scattering them everywhere. Then the tornado would cease to spin, and the dust would disperse in the air, fall and settle on the ground slowly.

Sayeed woke up, moved his head away from the edge of the window, wiped his eyes with his *gutra*, and looked around the minibus. A few passengers were asleep. One was reading a magazine. The driver had his left hand on the wheel, rhythmically tapping the knob of the gear lever with the palm of his right hand to the tune he was humming, shaking his head slowly from side to side.

'We will be approaching the Hop Hopu village soon. If anyone wants to buy food, there is a good café over there. I do not recommend their chicken, but their lamb is good,' the driver said.

Everyone started to look out of the front windscreen of the minibus to see two rows of buildings far away, on either side of the stretch of straight road.

When they came closer to the buildings, the driver turned left off the main road, drove on a small dust track raising a cloud of dust, and stopped at a filling station which was painted green. There were four petrol pumps mounted on an elevated wall, in the middle of the yard. A Yemeni wearing a kilt and a green checked cotton *gutra* came out of a small shed nearby and started filling the tank. The driver pushed his seat back, straightened his legs, and stretched his arms above his head.

One by one all the passengers got off the bus. Some started to cross the road to the café on the other side.

Sayeed and a few other passengers walked towards the grocery shop next to the filling station. The shop was a small mud hut, to the front of which a corrugated iron roof was fixed to give some shade. A big chest freezer stood across the entrance. Inside the shop there was a large refrigerator, and all around the walls, shelves were stacked with goods. There were tins of biscuits from China, cigarettes, and famous brand look-alike goods from the Far East: bottles of shampoo, perfume and other toiletries. The desert cooler which was fixed on the wall near the entrance to the shop was blowing cold humid air. A man was sleeping on the floor, on a plastic mat in the middle of the shop. Sayeed and three other passengers had to wake the shopkeeper up. Sayeed bought a bottle of lemonade, opened it with the bottle opener which was tied to a string attached to the counter. He rubbed off the neck of the bottle with his palm, and drank some of the contents. It was cool in the shade under the roof. Music from a radio came from the other side of the road, from the direction of the cafeteria. some of the passengers were standing outside, chatting loudly. At the filling station the driver was paying the Yemeni attendant.

Sayeed was not hungry, but he thought he should buy some food for later. He bought some dry cheese rolls and bananas. He took the polythene bag with his goods and walked towards the bus. The driver was not there. A few of the passengers were walking back from the café, and some were sitting crouched down in a circle in the shade of the filling station, talking while sipping their ice-cold drinks.

The sky was getting darker, and a wind started to blow, tossing discarded paper in the air. Sayeed got back into the minibus and sat down. Outside, the wind was getting stronger, and the passengers started to climb on. After a while the driver appeared, sat in his chair and blew the horn. The rest of the passengers came running, and when they were all on board the driver started the journey again.

The wind was getting stronger, and the desert all around was darkening. The passengers talked about a coming dust storm. Sayeed was beginning to get worried. 'Hope the road will not get covered with sand, and we will not get lost,' he thought, and looked at the sky which was beginning to turn orange. Far away to the right they could see a high tornado, and there were a few small ones forming and disintegrating all around them in the desert. The road began to get covered with blowing sand, which was hitting the windscreen and the other closed windows of the minibus. The driver had already closed all the air inlets, and turned off the fan. The windscreen wipers were turned on, and the dust storm was descending around them like a thick fog. The driver slowed down to about half his original speed. A spray of very fine sand was coming inside the bus and the passengers covered their noses with their head scarves and began to breathe through them. The driver had to slow down to almost a crawling speed as visibility was reduced to a few metres. He switched on the head lamps and was leaned forward over his steering wheel, crawling in second gear on the gradually disappearing road. There were no other vehicles on the road. The driver thought it would be unwise to carry on driving further in case the carburettor got blocked with dust. So he stopped the minibus on the kerb, switched off the engine and turned off the head lamps. He turned around to look at the worried passengers.

'God willing, this will not last very long,' he said with a smile. None of the passengers said anything.

'I hope no one will come and collide with our minibus,' he said and laughed. Some of the passengers started to look in both directions to see if any vehicles were coming.

The howling wind was getting stronger, and it began to shake the minibus. A fine layer of dust was settling on people's clothes, hair, and everything inside. The sun was hidden completely. Sayeed thought this was one of the worst sand storms that he had ever seen.

One of the passengers started sneezing continuously, his eyes were watering and he was having difficulty in breathing. He was blowing his nose constantly and making a groaning noise. Everyone looked worried, wishing the sand storm would cease.

It took more than an hour for the sand storm to slow down, and gradually the sky began to subside. The driver started the engine, switched on the head lamps and began to drive slowly. A few more vehicles with their head lamps on were coming in both directions, and the drivers flashed lights and blew horns when they passed each other. The sneezing passenger was better now, sneezing less frequently, but his eyes were still weeping.

When they came to the next town, most of the passengers got off. There were three left, including Sayeed. The other two passengers were going to a village a bit further than Sayeed's.

It was much clearer now, and the dust storm had almost passed. Everyone looked fatigued. By now, it was getting towards late afternoon. The driver had turned off the head lamps, and was driving fast. He had to take a few turnings on the way to Sayeed's village. The landmarks were becoming familiar to Sayeed. There had been many changes around this area since he had left the village, he thought.

The sun was going down like a blazing red ball over the palm trees and over the flat-roofed mud houses of his village, towards the west, on the horizon. It was a pleasing sight for Sayeed. No Abdul Mubarak to shout at him; no wicked children to tease him; no fast-moving, big cars, and no foreigners. It was a happy thought, and Sayeed felt relaxed.

'I visited your village a long time ago,' one of the other passengers said to Sayeed.

'I was born there, but I haven't been home for a few years. I have some land, and my brother is looking after it,' Sayeed said. The other passenger smiled. Sayeed wanted to tell him more about himself, where he worked, how much money he had saved, but he refrained.

Sayeed sat quietly with his chin over the back of the seat in front of him, and watched the driver turn the minibus towards his village. He could see it clearly now. The sun had fallen further towards the horizon, and it was below the top level of palm trees which were moving slowly in the wind.

The driver stopped the minibus just outside the village, and Sayeed collected his bundle from under the seat. He thanked the driver, said goodbye to everyone, got off the bus, and started to walk towards his village.

Chapter 5

It was a familiar sight. From the road where he was dropped, he walked down the slope, and under the bridge over the *wadi* which ran like a circle around the village, towards his brother's house.

Sayeed started to walk on the *wadi*, on the dust track. He was weary now, but happy. He was home at last. None of the hustle and bustle of the city, no noise of construction work, only the serenity of his quiet home village.

The sun was still visible through the leaves of the palm trees which were planted close to each other over most of the village. Dates were one of the village's main sources of income. Sayeed's slippers were getting covered with dust as they sank in the track. The borders of his ankle-length white *thorbe* were turning brown with dust. He walked fast, the sun in front of him and a lengthening shadow behind him, with his bundle over his right shoulder. He was looking either side of the bank to see whether there had been any changes since he had been away, or whether he could recognise any familiar houses.

Now and then he could see a thrown-away wheel, or smashed-up pieces of motor or broken-down and abandoned vehicles in the valley. Near to the bank of the *wadi* to the left were some old mud houses with flat roofs, now derelict. Sayeed could remember the time when a few families lived in those houses. Sayeed's old friend Yasser's parents had owned one of them. Yasser was about the same age as Sayeed, and when they were children they used to play on the rocks just outside the village. Yasser was a good tree-climber. He used to climb tall palms and bring down bundles of dates, then they used to sit in the shade and eat the semi-ripe fruit, and catapult the stones with their tongues. Yasser's parents were dead now, and Yasser had gone to the city. With no one to water the date palm trees, they were dead too. The sight of those houses brought back childhood memories for Sayeed, and he felt sad. Those were days that had gone, never to return.

Sayeed had to move to the side when a Toyota truck came fast from the direction he had left. A thick cloud of dust was shooting behind it. A young boy of about fifteen was driving it, and another young boy was sitting next to him. They were laughing and the ends of their checked red and white *gutra*s were waving in the wind, their bodies bobbing up and down with the bumping of the truck on the dust track. The village had certainly changed, Sayeed thought. Not many vehicles were around when Sayeed was here. When he was young it had been donkey carts that they rode.

There were some children playing outside a grocery shop which faced the bank of the *wadi* on his right. There were a few new buildings scattered around there, some were two or three storeys high and every house or block of flats had television antennae fixed to its roof. The children, all about ten years old, were playing with a football. They were too busy playing to notice the frail figure of Sayeed walking down below on the *wadi*. Their noise and the music that came from a radio in the grocery shop broke the silence.

After walking a bit further, Sayeed could see, beyond another bridge over the *wadi*, the palm trees of his brother's garden. The closely planted trees looked healthy with their lush greenery moving gently in the wind like a sea of leaves.

Sayeed passed under the bridge, and after pacing a few metres he turned left, and walked up the sloped path towards his brother's house. The date palm grove lay between the house and the road, connected by the bridge over the *wadi*, and one end of the bridge was near the far end of the palm grove. Towards the other side of the house was the land where Sayeed's brother grew vegetables, and behind the house were the pens for the sheep, goats and the few chicken which they bred, and near by the water well. The two-storey house was fairly big; Sayeed's brother's two wives and their children lived in it. From the front of the house which faced the *wadi*, one could see it stretching in either direction, and on the other side of it, further away from its bank, some new houses were under construction. During the day the *wadi* could be busy with traffic taking a short cut to the main road towards the city.

The sun was still high and the long shadow of the house fell towards the palm grove. A horse was tied to one of the bushes in front of the house. It was grazing on dried-up blades of grass, and when it heard Sayeed's footsteps it raised its head, and looked towards him.

One of Sayeed's sisters-in-law, Halima, the older and the first wife of his brother, Mustafa, was sitting outside on the ground, leaning against the wall of the house facing the palm grove. She was wearing a long black dress, and her hair was covered with a piece of black cloth. Her legs were stretched out before her, and on her thighs a small girl of about six was sitting cross-legged. The woman was grooming the child's hair by pinching a strand of hair between the nails of her thumb and forefinger, pulling the nits along its length; then she would place the nits on the nail of one thumb, and crush them with the nail of the other thumb, making a crackling sound, and this continued. Now and then she would part the child's hair and examine the hair closely for lice, and when she found one, she would pick it up and crush it again between her two thumb nails. They were in the shadow of the house, and it was getting difficult to make out what she was doing. When the horse suddenly moved, Halima looked up to see who was there. At first she did not recognise the silhouetted figure of a man coming towards the house. She quickly covered her face with her veil. Then she recognised the walk, and lifted the veil and threw it over her head. Sayeed came walking towards her. She pushed the child away slowly, and twisted her body to the left, put both hands on the sand, pressing them down hard, bent her knees, and with a slight struggle, stood up.

A thin smile came over Halima's face. It had been a few years since Sayeed left the village, and she had missed him, especially after the second wife came and Mustafa's attention turned more towards her. She was getting isolated in her own house. The children and the animals and the farming kept her busy, but she did not have many interests, or friends. Sayeed had been a great help to her when he had lived with them, but he went to the city a few months after the new wife was brought, and she was lonely among her own family.

'Salaam alaykum, Halima,' Sayeed said.

'Wa-alaykum is-salaam, Sayeed,' Halima replied, straightening her dress, and brushing the sand off it. She cleared her throat, and spat on the sand.

'How are you, Halima?' Sayeed asked affectionately.

'I am fine,' she said, and her animated expression changed. Her smile was reduced to a thoughtful frown, and she looked down on the child and started to stroke her head. Sayeed had left home when the child was only a year old, so she had only heard about Sayeed up to now. The child was trying to hide behind Halima's skirt and Sayeed put his hand in his pocket, took out some sweets and held them towards her. A little hand stretched out, took the sweets, and a smile came from the little face peeping out behind Halima's skirt.

'This is your Uncle Sayeed. Come and thank him for the sweets,' Halima said, and she tried to pull the child out. Sayeed said not to bother her, and that, given time, she would get used to him.

'How are you, Sayeed?' Halima asked him again.

'Oh, I am fine.'

'How is the city?'

'Very busy. I do not like it.'

'Have you earned a lot of money?'

'No, but I have saved some.'

'Are you going to be here long? We would like you to stay for a long time. We haven't seen you for so long.'

'I have only a few days' leave, so I have to go back soon. It is nice to be back home. It is so different. The city is like a foreign land. Many foreigners work there.

Even our people who live in the city are different. I prefer the village, it's my home,' Sayeed said.

There were a few children playing in the palm grove, and when Sayeed and Halima walked over, they stopped and came running towards them. They were all Mustafa's children, and some had recognised their uncle. Sayeed had a broad smile on his face. He did not say anything, but looked at their dust-covered faces and nodded his head. Then he tried to touch their heads. There was a little girl about four years old, she was the child of Mustafa's second wife, Akila. She wore a short green dress, and was looking at Sayeed with a big smile on her face. All the children were barefooted.

'That cheeky little one is Akila's,' Halima said.

'She's cute,' said Sayeed, taking some sweets out of his pocket and giving them to her. She took them and looked at the other children's faces, and gave a loud laugh. Sayeed gave sweets to the other children as well.

'I think we should go in now. It's getting dark,' Halima said.

The children were exchanging sweets and laughing.

'Go and drive the animals to the pens before it gets too dark, and fill up their troughs and give them some grass,' Halima said to the children. Then they all began to walk towards the back of the house, towards the animal pens.

'Let us go in,' Halima said, and started to walk towards the front of the house. They climbed two steps on to the verandah. In a corner of the floor, Mustafa was sleeping. The sound of footsteps woke him. He sat up, rubbed his eyes with the backs of his hands, and saw Sayeed.

'Ah, Sayeed!' he exclaimed.

'Salaam alaykum,' Sayeed said.

'Wa-alaykum is-salaam, Sayeed,' answered Mustafa. 'Kayf haalak?'

'Al-hamdulillah, shukran.'

Sayeed and Halima sat on the floor near Mustafa.

'So, how is life in the big city?'

'I don't like it. We have to live like paupers there. I live in a small hut in the desert. I haven't got enough money to get decent accommodation. The foreigners are every-where, and our people let all the houses and the flats to them because they can get good money. So we cannot get decent places,' Sayeed said.

'You have to put up with a bit of hardship if you want to earn some money, and I hope they pay you good money,' Mustafa said.

'The money is not too bad. I manage to save some as well. All my food is free from the hospital.'

'Did you buy some gold for me?' Halima asked, with a smile.

'Yes, I got a pair of bangles for you, and another for Akila,' said Sayeed.

'I hope my pair is different from hers.'

'Yes, yes,' Sayeed said, and he started to open the bundle.

'This one likes her very much,' Halima said, nodding towards Mustafa. 'She is a young chick, whereas I am an old goat now. You should see the dresses she wears for him! Always putting make-up on her face, and the perfume . . . upstairs smells like a harem!'

Mustafa gave an embarrassed smile, looked at Sayeed, then away towards the *wadi*, then at the horse.

'I must take the horse to the barn. Where are the children?' he asked, getting up.

Sayeed heard footsteps, and someone turning the

53

electric lights on inside the house. Then a pleasant smell reached his nostrils. He looked towards the door. Akila came towards him, and turned on the light in the verandah. She was surprised to see Sayeed. They exchanged greetings, and Akila said how glad she was to see him. He gave her the bangles, and she thanked him. Mustafa looked at Sayeed and then at Halima's frowning face. Halima was getting up. Mustafa walked from the verandah into the front yard.

'I am going to take the horse to the barn, and give him some water. Kill a few chickens and we will have a feast tonight!' he said, turning towards Halima.

'Kill chickens! Kill chickens! Who is going to do that? I am the servant here, am I?' Halima asked.

'I will kill the chickens,' Sayeed said.

With a gentle smile on her face, Akila said she would cook the rice.

'Oh, the lady will cook the rice. The easy work! I will have to cook the chicken. This is slavery!' Halima went on.

'Let us make a nice meal for our brother-in-law, let us make him happy and welcome,' Akila said in a slow, gentle voice.

'Hmm, let us go and get these chickens. You kill them, and I will pluck them,' Halima said to Sayeed.

Akila went to the kitchen and started to cook the rice. Sayeed went round to the back of the house with Halima. They turned the outside lights on. The children were still busy trying to drive the animals back into the pen. Sayeed caught three chickens with the help of the children. Halima brought a long sharp knife from the kitchen. Sayeed took the knife from Halima, said a prayer and cut the heads off the chickens, then threw them away towards the rubbish pit near the vegetable fields. The children were happy; they found it amusing to watch the headless fluttering chickens. When the chickens had become still, everyone helped to pluck them, and Halima cooked them.

The children straightened the carpet in the sitting room, and arranged the square-shaped, pillow-like cushions against the wall. Akila, with the help of two boys, brought the large circular enamel plate filled with rice, and placed it in the middle of the carpet. Halima brought a large saucepan filled with chicken, and laid the chicken on top of the rice.

They all sat around this large plate, in a circle, with Mustafa and Sayeed leaning their backs against the walls, and their left elbows resting on the cushions. They rolled up their right sleeves, dug their fingers into the rice, took a handful and squashed it into a cigar-shaped bundle, then put it in their mouths. The rice was arranged in several layers. Between each layer were different kinds of nuts and spices. There were dried limes cooked with rice, now soft and smooth, and filled with pleasant warm, sour liquid. The chicken smelled good; its oily skin glistening brown with green herbs sprinkled over it made everyone hungry. They ate heartily and washed their food down with water.

'I am lucky I have two good wives, and they can both cook well,' Mustafa said. They all laughed.

After the meal, Akila and her little daughter went upstairs, and the other children went to their rooms on the ground floor. Mustafa lit a cigarette, and Halima started to do the washing-up.

It was nearly midnight when Sayeed went outside. The wind was blowing slowly, and he could hear the rustling noise of the palm leaves. It was pitch dark. A restless noise came from the animal pens. The night was beginning to get cold. Sayeed walked towards the palm grove. He thought he knew every tree, and every stone that was there. It was so dark, but he knew his way around the palm grove. He went to the middle, and sat with his back against a tree. The rough remnants of the palm leaves with their cut edges pointing upwards on the trunk made Sayeed's back prickly. He looked up. The palm leaves silhouetted against the starry sky were gently swaying in the wind. He could hear the flutter of birds sleeping in the trees. He could smell the jasmine, and the nocturnal flowers. A rattling noise came from the house where Halima was doing the washing-up. How nice it is to be back home, he thought. The quiet calm life of the village.

A few dew drops fell on him. He thought how lonely he was. Even though he had friends at the hospital, there was no one close to him. Mustafa was looking for him. They had arranged Sayeed's old room for him on the ground floor. Mustafa came on to the verandah and looked around. He could not see anything.

'Sayeed!' Mustafa called.

'Yes, I am coming,' Sayeed's voice came from the palm grove.

Chapter 6

When Sayeed woke up, it was getting lighter, and the
cockerels had started crowing. It had been a warm night,
and he was sweating. Sayeed was feeling very thirsty, but
he did not get up for a glass of water in case he woke
anyone else. He had slept well, and peacefully, in his
familiar old room. The snores and the sleep talk of others
had woken him up once during the night, but he was
tired after his long journey and had had no problem
getting back to sleep.

Two of Mustafa's older boys were sharing the room
with Sayeed. They were sleeping on their foam mat-
tresses on either side of the door. Sayeed had been given
a space below the wide double window on the opposite
side of the door.

Sayeed lay on his mattress and looked around the
room which was still in semi-darkness, with its unplas-
tered rugged clay wall, now with a few pictures and a
large Japanese calendar hanging on it, and the mud
ceiling with five crooked wooden beams across it. This
had been his home for many years, and brought back
many memories. Sayeed lifted his head and ran his hand
over the foam pillow. The pillow case was wet with
sweat. He turned over the pillow, put his head on it,
and looked towards the mud wall. He ran his hand over

it, and felt a piece of straw. He loosened the piece of straw, pulled it out, and crumbled it between his thumb and his forefinger, and pressed the powdered straw back into a crack in the wall.

Both boys were fast asleep. One of them was bent like an arc with his hands tucked between his thighs, and was facing the wall; the other had rolled off the foam mattress, his arms stretched above his head and his legs spread wide.

Mustafa and Akila and their little girl were sleeping upstairs, and the rest were sleeping downstairs. It was all quiet except for the occasional snore and the rustling of the animals in their pens.

It was still fairly dark. Sayeed picked a large piece of sand from the wall and started rolling it between his forefinger and his thumb and felt the roughness of its edges. He started thinking about his childhood. He remembered his father, mother, grandparents, and the little sister who had died when she was about five years old. He could still remember their faces, even though they were a bit hazy when he first thought of them. With a little concentration he could visualise them so vividly.

Everyone said his grandfather was a very strong person. He had owned properties in the village, and had had a large herd of camels. People respected him. He looked fierce, and could gallop a horse without a saddle and no one could catch him. He had had several wives. They all had their own houses, and he visited each in turn. All the wives and children were happy. Then the raiders came, and they took away the camels, and took possession of some of his property. He could not do anything about it, because the raiders became the rulers, and he was left with only one house where his favourite wife lived. She was Sayeed's grandmother. Some of his wives were killed or taken by the raiders. Children were killed too. The villagers who had resisted were killed. But Sayeed's grandfather made peace with the new rulers, and he was allowed to keep one property, which was where Mustafa was living now.

Sayeed's father was the only child his grandmother had. He grew up to be a gentle person, and was married to only one woman. This was unusual in the village then when everyone had more than one wife. She liked her soft-spoken, shy husband. She was very beautiful, and a very kind person too. Sayeed's father loved her very much, and did not allow her to do any work around the house or on the farm. He had servants employed to do everything. Everyone liked her. But she died young, a year after the death of her little daughter. Sayeed was only eight years old then. His father never married again, and it seemed he lost the will to live, His health deteriorated and he did not have any wish to earn any money. The income they had received from the farm had dropped, and they had to dismiss all the servants. So, they became poor, and the two brothers had to work hard on the farm.

The grandparents had died before Sayeed's father's death. He could not remember the details, but he remembered that there were more people at his grandfather's funeral than at his grandmother's. His mother's was the saddest. Every woman in the village came to see her body, some cried very loudly, and every time they cried, Sayeed cried too. But Mustafa was silent. There were tears in his eyes, but he did not cry. Only a very few people came to Sayeed's little sister's funeral. His mother cried constantly for days, and his father cried too. His father carried the body in his arms to a faraway place in the desert, and his mother followed him, wailing loudly. Mustafa and Sayeed followed them. They buried her there in the dry, dusty, rugged desert.

A few years after his mother's death, his father died too. He could remember the sight of his father's body, lying on the mat, in his room, with his mouth slightly open, and his eyes cloudy, looking towards the ceiling. There were flies on his eyes, and on the inside of his mouth. It was around midday. Sayeed and Mustafa had come back from a neighbour's farm where they had been working all morning. Before they left for the farm, they thought their father, who had been unwell the previous night, was sleeping.

There was a sickly, pungent smell in the room. That same afternoon, his father's friends and neighbours took the body on a home-made stretcher, covered with a thin white sheet, for the burial.

The sun was going down, and it was very hot, that day in the late summer. They had taken the body far away into the desert, to the other side of the big rock where everyone buried their dead ones. They had placed the body in the grave, taken the white sheet off, and filled the grave with the rocky soil. Sayeed watched his father's face being covered with sand, dust, and rocks, and a fine cloud of dust rose from the grave.

Everyone had started to walk back to the village in silence. The adults were walking fast. Mustafa came last, walking behind Sayeed. Mustafa's tear-filled eyes were watching his own dust-covered bare feet moving slowly, trying to avoid the sharp stones. Sayeed stopped and looked back at his brother. Mustafa stopped and wrapped his arms around his chest. Sayeed took one of

Mustafa's hands, and they both looked at the adults walking away in the distance. All around them was the big empty desert, and behind them was the big rock.

Sayeed felt tears in his eyes. He placed the end of his forefinger near one eye, caught a tear on the tip of his finger, and placed the glistening drop on the mud wall. It was absorbed quickly, and left a small wet mark which was soon hardly visible.

The boys in the room were still asleep but it was getting lighter. Sayeed was feeling very thirsty. Then he heard a noise in the kitchen. He got up, opened the sliding windows of clouded glass, and looked outside. The dawn was breaking, but the sun was not up yet. The animals were stirring in their pens. Sayeed closed the window slowly, tiptoed out of the room, and went to the kitchen. Halima was getting ready to cook breakfast.

'Sabaah il-khayr,' Sayeed said.

'Sabaah in-nuwr, Sayeed. Did you sleep well?'

'Yes, I did. And did you, Halima?'

'I don't sleep well these days. The children. That man upstairs. I hear them sometimes. She laughs! Oh, I wish I could die!'

'Now, now, do not speak like that. Think of the children.'

'Yes. They are my life.' A smile came to Halima's face. 'Let us not talk about my problems. I will make you a nice breakfast. Why don't you go and have your wash and get ready for prayer?'

'All right, Halima. Did you pray?'

'No, I am going soon.'

Sayeed went out of the kitchen and into the back garden.

'Oh, Sayeed, can you start up the water pump. The plants must be watered soon,' Halima said.

Sayeed went to the shed where the water pump was, and switched it on. It started hesitantly, pumping out water through a large rubber hose which poured into a square concrete tank nearby. The tank was already full of water, and its overflow poured water into a drain which took it to the farm and the animal houses. Sayeed dipped his fingers in the water tank, and pulled them out quickly. It was cold. The water was clear, bubbles were forming and bursting as the water poured out of the pump into the tank. Sayeed cupped his hands together, took some water, and washed his face. He filled his mouth with water, rinsed it, then took a toothbrush stick out of his top breast pocket, and cleaned his teeth. He hurried inside, where Mustafa and the boys were ready for prayers. They prayed in the sitting-room, the wives and the girls in their own rooms. After the prayers, Sayeed went out to the garden again.

The noise of the water pump was louder and more rhythmic now. The birds that had perched on the trees during the night were noisy. They were flying everywhere and some had gathered near the animal pens. The goats were bleating and the chickens were crowing. A strong smell came from the animal houses which were next to the vegetable garden. The goats were shaking their ears, tails and heads, to drive away the storming flies. Sayeed looked towards the house. A few children were coming towards the water tank. Sayeed wanted to look over the farm, and especially his piece of land. He passed the animal house and walked towards the vegetable patch. He remembered the years he had spent, labouring on this land. Those were the days of hard work for little money. Now, he did not have to work that hard. Life at the hospital was much easier, he thought. He wondered how Mustafa's family was managing with only the income from this farm. Still, the cost of living in the village was low compared with the city, Sayeed decided.

He walked on the wet banks of the vegetable farm, watching the water flowing, bathing the stems and leaves of the plants, and being absorbed back into the earth. It was a fresh morning with the smell of dampness that came from the soil.

Sayeed was glad he could help his brother by letting him farm on his part of the land as well. His father had left the house to Mustafa, but a large proportion of the land to Sayeed.

Two of the boys were milking the goats. Sayeed watched them for a little while, then went back to the kitchen. It was full of smoke, and the cooking smell made Sayeed hungry.

'It's almost ready. As soon as the boys come back from the shop with bread, we can eat,' Halima said.

Everyone was up and busy inside the house. Akila came downstairs with her little daughter, and went towards the water tank to wash her. Mustafa was in the sitting-room drinking a glass of goat's milk and smoking a cigarette.

'Ah, Sayeed. Do you want some goat's milk?'

'I think I would rather have some tea.'

'This is fresh goat's milk. One of the boys brought some for me. It's warm still, and it's good for you.'

'All right then, just a little,' Sayeed said.

Mustafa poured some milk from the jug into a glass, and gave it to Sayeed. He used to drink goat's milk every day when he lived there. Since he'd gone to the city he'd got used to drinking a hot cup of tea with the others in the laboratory. Sayeed picked up the glass of frothing milk, and with his forefinger removed some floating goat's hair, and drank the lukewarm, unboiled milk.

Soon breakfast was ready. The leftover chicken from the previous night was warmed up. There were boiled eggs, home-made cheese, black olives, and fresh peta bread that the boys had brought from the shop nearby. They ate greedily, and drank glasses of goat's milk. Akila's little girl was refusing to eat the boiled eggs, but Halima's girl ate everything without a fuss.

It started to get warm inside. Outside, the sun was becoming bright and intense.

Chapter 7

After breakfast Mustafa and Sayeed took their glasses of tea, with the tea bags and the strings still in them, on to the verandah. The sun was bathing the bushes in front of the house, and the *wadi*, and the bank on the other side of the *wadi*, and the houses there. The palm grove to the right, its bright fronds swaying in the slight breeze, and the green bushes at the end of the palm grove and on the bank of the *wadi* shone in the bright sunlight.

They sat with their backs against the wall on the blue plastic mat. There were red velvet cushions, patterned with large yellow flowers, to rest their elbows on. They put the steaming-hot glasses of tea, filled to the brim, on the mat, slowly, trying not to spill any. Mustafa put his hand in his pocket, and took out a box of matches, and a packet of Rothmans.

'You still do not smoke?' Mustafa asked.

'No.'

'Good. It's a very bad habit,' Mustafa said, and he gave a broad grin, showing his few leftover teeth. He ran his tongue over his lips, took a cigarette out of the packet, tapped the filter end on the nail of his left thumb, placed the cigarette between his lips, and lit it. Then he took a deep breath, and exhaled it through his nose and mouth at the same time. With eyes still tearful, he picked up the glass of tea and sipped a mouthful, the cigarette smoke still coming out of his nose.

'Hmm. Nice. Bit more sugar would made it much better,' Mustafa said. 'Did the women tell you anything about a marriage proposal for you?'

'No.'

'Well, we would like to arrange a marriage for you.'

'What?' Sayeed laughed. 'I don't want a woman. I'm quite happy as I am.'

'There is a woman in the village called Latifa. We have heard that she is a good woman. Akila knows her, not very well though, but she says no one says anything bad about her,' Mustafa told him.

'I don't think I will ever marry.'

'She is not bad looking, Akila says. Her parents are still alive, and she lives with them, along with her child,' Mustafa said.

'She was married then?' Sayeed laughed. 'And she has a child too. This is a joke. Isn't it?'

'No, no. It is no joke. She is still young, and her child is very small. You are not young yourself any more, and it's not easy to find a woman at your age. We don't know whether she would agree to marry you anyway, but one thing is certain, you do not need a big dowry for her!'

Sayeed did not say anything. He picked up his glass of tea, sipping it slowly. He wiped his mouth with the back of his hand, put the glass on the mat, and looked outside. It was beginning to get very hot. He wiped his face with the end of his *gutra*, turned his hand over, and looked at the wrinkled dark skin. Then he looked at the back of the other hand, and turned both hands over, and bent the fingers inwards, looked at the long, dirt-filled nails. His hands had been muscular, not very long ago. He

66

remembered his father's hands. They were muscular, and strong. But as Sayeed grew up, and his father grew older, he had noticed that his father's skin started to get shiny, and later to wrinkle up.

He thought that he was too old to get married. There was a time when he thought of women. That was when he was young. But he had been busy working hard on the farm, and he had had to look after Mustafa too. There had been no one to help. It had been a hard life then, and still was a hard life, even now.

He looked at Mustafa. He was resting his left elbow on the square cushion, his left leg bent and resting on the mat, his right knee up. His right arm with the cigarette between his fingers was resting on that knee.

'Well, what do you think?' Mustafa asked.

'I am not young any more. I do not need a woman.'

'I suggest you think about this a bit more seriously. You are my elder brother, so I cannot tell you what to do. But you are my only brother, and I would like you to be happy. Man is no man without a woman. Look, I have two!' Mustafa laughed.

'I am getting old now.'

'Ahk! Rubbish! Look at Ali Suweri. You remember Ali Suweri in the village, don't you? He must be nearly seventy years old now. He dyes his hair and his beard red with henna, and he got married again last week! The woman is younger than Akila. Lucky man he is. I really envy him.'

'I like a peaceful life. I do not have to think about anyone. I go where I want, when I want, and when I buy anything I do not have to share it with anyone. I am free. I like children, but they do not seem to like me.'

'That's because you are too soft with them, you let

67

them make fun of you. You were tough when you were young. You used to fight with the other boys, and with me too!' Mustafa said.

'Well, I don't know. I am happy as I am. Please don't bother me. I made up my mind a long time ago. Women are pretty before they get married, but soon after childbirth they get fat and ugly. They are all the same, they talk too much, and nag their husbands. I am free now, and I will stay free!'

'There's no harm in going to see her, is there? You might not be able to see her face, but at least you could see her shape. Her parents are very nice, farming folks, like us. The father had only one wife, Latifa's mother. This woman's child is a pretty little thing.'

'Have you been to see them recently?'

'Only yesterday. Akila said that I should go and meet the parents, and ask about you.'

'What? You should not have done that!' said Sayeed angrily.

'Don't get angry. As soon as we knew you were coming here, we thought of finding someone for you, and Akila mentioned this girl.'

'You never asked me!'

'I am asking you now. You can forget about it if you want, but we have arranged for you to go and see them this evening.'

'I am not going anywhere. I don't want any woman,' Sayeed said, raising his voice, and pointing his index finger at Mustafa. He got up, stepped off the verandah into the front yard, and started walking towards the date palm grove.

'We must go this afternoon. It's all been arranged. Five o'clock this afternoon,' Mustafa said in a loud voice,

68

getting up and following Sayeed, who was walking quickly away from the house.

'What a stupid man. I give up. He does not listen to anyone. He does not know what he is missing,' Mustafa said, throwing his arms in the air. 'Women are lovely. I wish I could get another young one. Mind you, I am getting a bit old myself. So what? Perhaps I should get another one quickly. But I don't want any more children.' Mustafa was muttering to himself. He came back, sat on the mat on the verandah, emptied the last drop of tea in the glass, lit a new cigarette, and yelled to Halima for another glass of tea.

Sayeed walked quickly towards the date palm grove, without looking back. The tall trees with their scaly-looking brown stumps of old leaf bases pointing upwards gave some shade from the hot sun. In a corner of the grove, near the fence towards the bridge connecting the two banks of the *wadi*, there was a bushy area with hibiscus, lemon, and pomegranate trees all around, and desert pines planted all around the fence. In this isolated corner young palm trees grew, their long, dark, lustrous green leaves almost touching the ground. The trees were laden with bundles of orange dates. Tall grass and mimosa plants with their tiny, sharp thorns covered the slightly damp, dark brown soil. Every other day the date palm grove was watered. The salty desert water was filtered through several banks of soil before it reached this corner. These banks, which partitioned the palm grove into large square fields, held water for a while for the palm trees to absorb, and were used as footpaths for easy access to different parts of the palm grove. Once the ripe dates were cut and brought down, they were separated and graded. Then traders gave a good price for them. The leftover branches, like porcupines, were left lying in the palm grove. Animal waste was used as manure on the palm grove, and this corner, which was at a lower level than the rest, got most of the nutrients, since the water from other parts of the palm grove accumulated there. So any seed which fell on this corner grew freely.

Sayeed came walking through the palm grove into this serene corner, and sat with his back against a hibiscus tree. He stretched his legs. 'It is not his business to organise my life,' he muttered. He could hear, like an echo, the conversation that he had had with Mustafa.

He was still angry. The palm grove was shady, but the heat was getting intense, and the dense growth made it humid. Sayeed took his *gutra* ends and wiped the sweat from his forehead and neck. He could hear the rhythmic thump of a water pump in the distance. Children were playing somewhere. They sounded very faint. They must be far away at the other end of the garden, on the other side of the house, or at their neighbour's, Sayeed thought. He heard a little girl crying. It could be Akila's little daughter getting teased by other children, he thought.

Sayeed lay down on the grass, under the shade of the lemon trees with their lush green leaves, laden with long green lemons. It was very peaceful. He raised his hand, picked a lemon, and pressed his thumb nail on its skin. Fragrant juice splattered on his nail. He raised the lemon to his nose, smelled the broken skin, and rubbed it against his face.

Mustafa said the woman was still young. She had been married for less than three years when her husband died, and Akila had said that she was very beautiful. Sayeed rubbed the lemon on his lips, and on his nose, and breathed in the fresh smell.

Akila wore nice perfume. Most women wore perfume. It made them more attractive. They had long black hair. After a bath when they dried their hair the smell of the soap stayed with them for a long time.

'I wonder what it is like to feel their skin,' Sayeed mused. How it would feel to put his face on a woman's face, to put his body on a woman's body, just to touch a woman's hand, he could not imagine.

'Ahk. I must not think these things. I am too old now,' Sayeed mumbled, and bit the lemon. The bitter taste of it made his eyes water. He squinted, swallowed the juice slowly, and looked around. The plants and their leaves were motionless now. There was no wind. He could hear a motor vehicle driving fast in the *wadi* below, and he could see the bridge through the gaps between the trees. It was Friday, a holiday for everyone. 'Supposing I decide to marry this woman, and supposing she agrees, where am I going to live? This house is not big enough for another family, and even if it were big, the women would only start to fight with each other. And my job is in the city. This farm is not big enough even for a single family. Will she come to the city? Life in the city is not that comfortable. The huts are small and close together. Perhaps I could get a bigger hut, or make mine bigger. But it is too hot, and dusty, and there's not enough water, not enough space for children to play. It is too crowded with poor families who have migrated to the city to make a better living. It is not a comfortable life at all. But the money is good. You can find a job easily, and buy what you want.'

Sayeed looked at the pomegranate trees which were

bearing fruit, and the red hibiscus flowers with their petals silhouetted against the sunlight filtering through the green leaves in the bush. It was quiet. Sayeed felt very sleepy. He did not feel angry any more. He felt relaxed and happy, and he did not know why. Perhaps because he was back home, and he was with his own people. No Abdul Mubarak to shout at him. No children to abuse him. Many a time in the past he had come to this corner of the palm grove, when he had problems or worries, and contemplated solutions. He turned on his side, put the palm of his hand under his head, and in no time was fast asleep.

Quietly, butterflies flew from flower to flower, gently shaking their wings. The ants were busy gathering the fallen pollen, and filing along a set path down to their houses below in the earth. A gently humming fly came to land on Sayeed's mouth, and he automatically moved his hand and drove the fly away, but he did not wake up.

He slept soundly in the shade, without any disturbance. When he woke up he felt unusually happy, and excited. He saw the green leaves, the red flowers, the pomegranates and the small bushes moving slowly from side to side in the slight breeze. He had been sweating a little. He wiped his face and his hands with his *gutra*.

He tried to remember the pleasant dream that he had had a few minutes before. It was a beautiful woman's face that kept appearing in his mind. It was like a face that he had seen in a magazine in the hospital. But she was in a house, on a balcony, on the first floor. The house had a high wall around it, and a big wide iron gate which was locked. The woman was without a veil, and she wore a white dress without any sleeves. Her fair face, neck and bare hands were beautiful. Sayeed was standing outside the wall on the other side of the road. When the woman saw him, she smiled. Sayeed smiled back, and looked away. He started to walk away. Then he stopped, and looked at the balcony. The woman was smiling still, and he smiled again. He looked around. There was no one else. Sayeed was happy. Then he had woken up. He was sad that he had woken up so suddenly, before he had finished the dream. His body was reacting to the dream, and he looked around to see whether anyone was looking. No one was to be seen, and he turned on his belly and watched the ants walking busily and inquisitively, investigating everything near their path, following each other. He cleared his throat, formed a large ball of sputum in his mouth, and spat it in the ants' path. It fell on a dry leaf nearby. The leaf shook a little, and the ants moved away quickly. When it was quiet, one by one the ants started to walk towards the blob of sputum, and soon they were standing side by side all around it, drinking. Sayeed spat again, and this time it fell on the soft powdered soil. It became a ball of wet sand and started rolling down the small slope.

Two flies were mating in the shade on a grass leaf, their hind sides attached, their wings fluttering intermittently. Sayeed shook the leaf, and the flies fell on to another leaf below, but stayed attached, and their wings started fluttering faster to balance each other.

'That is nature,' Sayeed thought.

He could still hear Mustafa's words: 'Man is no man without a woman.'

He heard noises in the *wadi* below. He sat up and looked through the gaps between the trees. A big yellow bus stood there, full of South Koreans who had come out to the village for a picnic on their day off. The door of the bus was open, and the grey-uniformed Koreans were getting off, talking loudly, and spreading out in groups, carrying bottles of water and some parcels.

'If I ignore this opportunity, Mustafa and the others will never again try to find me a woman. After all, if everyone says it is for my good, I cannot ignore them. There is no harm in going to see her anyway,' he thought.

He stood up, shook the sand from his *thorbe*, adjusted his *gutra*, went towards a short date palm tree, picked up a few ripe dates, and started eating them. He was feeling very thirsty. A young boy on a horse went galloping very fast on the *wadi* below. Sayeed started to walk towards the house.

Chapter 8

The children were not back yet. Mustafa was sleeping on the verandah. It was almost midday, and the heat was intense.

Sayeed walked towards the back of the house. Akila was washing clothes in a large green plastic basin, near the water pump. She looked at Sayeed and smiled. 'Every day I have to wash a lot of clothes,' Akila said, getting up and shaking the water off her hands, and wiping them on her long green skirt, her gold bangles tinkling. 'They dirty their clothes so badly, it is difficult to wash them.' She raised her right hand and wiped the sweat off her forehead with the long sleeve of her blouse.

'Children are like that. When Mustafa was young he wore the same clothes for many days. He used to say it was no use washing them because they only got dirty again,' Sayeed said, smiling.

'I must finish this washing quickly, and give Halima a hand with the cooking. She always complains that I don't help her in the kitchen,' Akila said, as she sat down again.

'Why doesn't Halima like you?'

'I don't know. Perhaps she is jealous, or perhaps she thinks she is getting old,' said Akila in a whisper, and giggled with her shoulders shaking, looking towards the kitchen door to see whether Halima was watching.

'She is older than you are, but she is not old, is she?'

Akila did not say anything. She continued washing the clothes, with a smile on her face.

'Please treat her like a sister. You know she hasn't got anywhere to go.'

'I do, I do. But she does not give me a chance. She is always sarcastic and angry.'

Sayeed started to walk towards the back door.

'What do you think about it?'

Sayeed stopped, and turned around. 'About what?'

'Mustafa said you were angry this morning.'

'Ah, yes. I don't know really.' Sayeed smiled.

'She is not bad. I know her. Any man would be lucky to have her,' Akila said, and she gave a big laugh.

Sayeed was embarrassed. He looked down, and started kicking the sand with the tip of his right slipper.

'There's no harm in going to see the family,' Akila said softly.

'You all seem to think I should get married.'

'We do not want to see you getting old and not having anyone to look after you. Please, brother, listen to us. This will make you happy, and make us happy too.'

Sayeed did not say anything for a moment. He looked towards the kitchen. There was no one to be seen. He heard the sound of cooking pots being moved about. He looked at Akila who was standing with her hands covered in white soap suds with tiny bubbles bursting constantly. She had a serious expression on her face, with supplicating eyes.

'Well, what time did Mustafa say we have to go there?' Sayeed asked with a smile.

'That's good,' Akila said approvingly, and she sat down again to her washing.

Sayeed walked through the back door into the kitchen. It was dark inside. He went directly to the kitchen sink, turned on the cold water tap, held his mouth under it, and drank several gulps of slightly warm water. He splashed some water all over his face, took the *gutra* off, and held his head under running water. It was soothing. Halima was sitting on the floor, cutting meat from bones, putting the small sticky pieces into a large aluminium pot coated with hard black soot.

She pouted, raised her eyebrows, and started giggling. Sayeed gave a slight cough, took a deep breath, and gave her a shy smile.

'Well, what do you think?'

'I don't know,' Sayeed said, and he crouched near her with his back towards the door.

'Move to the side, so I will not cut my fingers,' Halima said.

He moved and crouched down again, next to Halima, and picked up some dry curved onion skins, and started splitting them.

'You would like to! Wouldn't you?' she laughed.

Sayeed smiled, wiped the corner of his mouth with the back of his hand, and looked at the back garden. The kitchen door was slightly ajar, and he could see only the light brown sand in the yard in the blazing heat, and part of the animal pen.

'You men are all the same. You want only one thing. It's no good pretending that you don't like it. Might as well get everything sorted out soon. Where are you going to stay? There is no room here. You can see that, can't you? That idiot made this house crowded. I hope and pray he will become impotent one day.'

'Where is he?'

'Where do you think? Sleeping on the verandah. Women and children have to work, and he sleeps. He is a lazy good-for-nothing.'

'Now, now, Halima, talking like that only makes you unhappy,' Sayeed said, getting up. 'Anyway, I don't know whether this woman will like me.'

'Ahk. Don't worry about that. She will have to like you. You are not bad looking. Her parents are old, and she will have to think about herself, and the child. It's not up to her mainly. If her parents agree, that's all there is to it. I did not have a choice, and neither did Akila. We will see. You men! All the same,' said Halima, shaking her head, and smiling. 'You did not tell me where you will stay if you get married.'

'I will have to take her to the city. I don't know whether she would like it, but that's where my work is. My hut may not be big enough. I might have to make it bigger.'

Sayeed walked on to the verandah. Mustafa was sleeping soundly on his back. Sayeed went inside, and walked into the room where he had slept that night. The mattress was still on the floor. A mirror hung on the wall, near the window. He looked at his face. His wet black hair and eyebrows were plastered against his skin. He puffed up his cheeks, examined his face, and cleaned his eyes with the end of his *gutra*. Then he smiled.

He went to the mattress, lifted it up, and kicked the under side to shake off the dust. He shook the pillow, and lay down.

The smell of cooking that came from the kitchen was

making Sayeed hungry. He felt slightly happy, but anxious at the same time. His hut was not big enough, and a woman from the village might not like the city. His thoughts were all mixed. He wondered what his colleagues would think: they would laugh, and everyone he knew would laugh. So what? They could not laugh for ever, he thought. It would only be for a short time. It might only be for a week. Then they would stop. What about the child? He was sure people would say bad things about the woman, but he was not worried. He could look after them both, and they would be good company for him. He could take them to *souk*s, and watch the woman haggle, and he could buy toys and sweets for the child. He would buy everything they asked for. He might have to be a bit strict with the child perhaps, otherwise she would want everything. 'Oh, what I am thinking? This might never happen,' he thought.

'Where are the children? The food is ready,' Halima said as she and Akila came into the room. Sayeed sat up.

'I don't know,' he said.

'Shall I get some houmous ready?' Akila asked.

'Yes, madam, always the easy work!'

'Don't be rotten, Halima,' Akila said.

All the children came in at the same time, as if they had smelled the food from the end of the garden. Some were covered with sand, on their bare legs, faces, hands, hair and clothes. Their dark brown skins were itchy with dried mud. Some were rubbing their skin on their clothes to wipe off the sand. Halima drove them towards the pump to get washed before the meal. Mustafa was up. He was sitting in his usual place in the sitting-room, ready to eat. Sayeed told him about his decision, and

Mustafa was both pleased and amused. Then Sayeed said that he did not have any clothes to wear, so Mustafa asked Akila to give Sayeed one of his white silk *thorbe*s.

They all had a good lunch. The adults discussed Sayeed's future. The small children did not know what the adults were talking about, but the older children listened carefully, watching the adults' faces, especially Sayeed's, to see their reactions. They would stop talking one minute, and burst out laughing, all at the same time. This made Sayeed disconcerted, but he was beginning to get used to it. He was thinking that he should have a shower and a shave, before he went to see this woman. Perhaps he would put on some of Mustafa's aftershave, he thought. While the others were talking, he drifted into deep thoughts about himself.

Mustafa started yawning. Akila brought some coffee, and the children went outside again. Sayeed leaned against the wall, and stretched his legs. Halima started clearing away, and Mustafa lit a cigarette. Everyone was content and sleepy, but a busy afternoon was ahead. In a few hours they had to go to Latifa's house.

'We will go in the pick-up,' Mustafa said

'Are you taking the children as well?' Halima asked.

'Ahk, woman, not children, this is adult business. We don't want little children wandering around disturbing us. Do we now?'

'There is a little girl there already,' Halima said.

'They can play with her later. Our lot are wild. Leave them here. The pick-up hasn't a lot of space at the front. I think I will sleep for a while before we go,' Mustafa said.

'No, you won't. If you do, I will throw a bucket of water on you. Go and have a wash. You could do with a shower. And see to the animals before we go. We don't know what time we will be back,' Halima said.

'What a woman! I hope, God willing, you will have better luck than me,' Mustafa said with a smile, and threw the cigarette butt out of the window.

Chapter 9

It was a busy afternoon for everyone. The women had their showers at the water pump, and they washed the little children at the same time. Then Sayeed and Mustafa had their showers, and shaved their cheeks and trimmed their beards. Sayeed got into Mustafa's silk *thorbe* and put on a clean white *gutra*, and a fairly new pair of slippers. Akila wore her bright red dress, and Halima her green one. Both women were helping each other to adjust their new dresses which reached down to their ankles. Their wet hair was difficult to comb. Akila's black hair was smooth, and not very long. She usually combed it twice a day. But Halima's hair was knotted. They put fresh henna patches on their feet and on their faces, and some make-up, and perfume. They kept smiling at each other, and at their images in the mirror, and they were happy and friendly.

The children were busy outside. The older ones were chasing the animals into their pens. Some were throwing food to them, others were filling the water containers.

Sayeed put on some of Mustafa's aftershave. Everyone was inspecting him, instructing him to make changes to the *gutra*, or adjust his *thorbe*, or comb his beard. It was a jovial atmosphere, and Sayeed had a constant smile on his face. He was beginning to enjoy this attention. Mustafa would burst into loud fits of laughter, but put on a serious face whenever Sayeed frowned at him.

The smell of perfume and aftershave was everywhere in the house. The rustling of dresses, pattering of slippers, and tapping of high heels moved from room to room, hurriedly. The older children were put in charge of feeding and looking after the little ones.

Mustafa went towards the back of the house where he had parked the truck, and drove it to the front, parked it there, left the engine running, and got out. 'The pick-up is ready!' he bellowed.

An older boy brought four chickens, two in each hand, with their legs tied together and the wings fluttering, and threw them into the back of the truck. The chickens started jumping up and down, still with their wings fluttering. The truck was shaking from side to side with the vibration of the engine, and a cloud of greyish smoke was coming out of the back. 'Good boy!' Mustafa said, thanking the boy who had brought the chickens, a present for the bride-to-be's parents.

Mustafa took a piece of rag, wiped the dust off the seats, and got into the driver's side. He accelerated several times with the pedal all the way down. The engine screeched, and belched out a continuous stream of smoke.

'Benzine is a bit low, but it should be enough for the trip,' Mustafa muttered.

Sayeed came to the verandah, adjusted his *gutra*, and walked towards the truck.

'Are they ready?' asked Mustafa, taking his foot off the accelerator.

'Yes, they are about to come out.'

'Be careful you don't get any grease on your *thorbe*,' Mustafa said with a smile on his face.

'Let the women sit in the middle, I will sit near the door,' said Sayeed.

The women, their heads and bodies completely covered with black veils, came towards the truck, high-heeled shoes tapping.

Sayeed opened the door, and the women got in. Akila first, next to Mustafa, and then Halima. Sayeed got in last, and shut the door.

Mustafa said a small prayer, took the hand brake off, and the truck rolled down the slope towards the *wadi*, and turned left. They started travelling slowly on the dust track. A thick cloud of dust had formed, and their house, the date palm grove, and the *wadi* behind had disappeared in the cloud. It was warm in the truck, the air-conditioning was still not blowing out cold air. The windows of the truck were kept shut to keep the dust and the heat out. The swaying truck was moving fairly fast, but still in a low gear, on the uneven dust track.

In front of them, the sun was setting. Its orange rays were falling on the windscreen. On their left was a large green palm grove belonging to one of the wealthy people in the village. He lived in a villa in the middle of the grove. On the bank, to their right, houses were scattered on the rugged, almost barren land.

Everyone was quiet. The women were sitting with their veils on, with sweaty faces. Akila was stroking the imitation gold handles of her shiny black leather handbag, and Halima was glancing at Akila and Mustafa now and then, and looking out through the window on the driver's side.

'It's very hot in here. Open a window,' Halima said.

'The dust will get in, and it's no good opening a window if you have the air-conditioning on,' Mustafa said.

'It's not cold yet. We will be dead by the time this air-conditioner starts to work. I can't breathe,' Halima persisted.

'All right. I will open it, and when the air-conditioner starts blowing cold air, I will close the window,' Mustafa said, opening the window on his side. A gush of hot air came in.

'This air-conditioner is getting worse. It takes a long time to blow out cold air. I think it needs some freon,' Mustafa said.

After driving for about a mile in the *wadi*, Mustafa turned the truck to the left, climbed on the bank of the *wadi*, and drove on a small track in the middle of a date palm grove. The decaying stumps of palm trees, and other fallen trees, were scattered on the white sand on both sides of the track. Towards the inside of the palm grove it looked dark where thick leaves cut out the light. The track was narrow, and the picket fences of dried palm leaf stalks tied up vertically with metal wires lined the track on both sides. The whole area was deserted. They could see the large orange ball of sun appearing and disappearing behind the trees to their right, as the truck moved slowly in the sand track.

They came to a small built-up section where a few single-storey houses were scattered over a large portion of the palm grove. Around each house was a similar fence of palm leaf stalk, and each had a large garden. The narrow tracks around them made it difficult for the wide truck to turn. Mustafa had to move his truck forward and reverse it several times before he managed to turn around.

'That's their home,' Akila said, pointing to a bungalow at the end of the small track.

'Yes, at last we are here. The air-conditioning is working now,' Halima said.

Mustafa mumbled something, and hit the air-conditioning outlet with his right hand. Everyone laughed. Sayeed straightened his *gutra*, and started flicking dust from his white *thorbe*.

'I can't see anyone outside,' Mustafa said.

'Are we early?' Akila asked.

'What's the time now?' Mustafa asked.

Akila looked at her gold watch and said it was nearly five o'clock.

'Well, we said about five. They must be inside,' Mustafa said, as he pulled into the front yard.

Sayeed was feeling very anxious, and his throat was dry. He coughed slightly, and swallowed some sputum to wet his throat. He felt like turning back and hurrying away before anyone from the house came out. Not only was he shy, he was annoyed too. It seemed his life was being organised by others, for his sake, for his good, as they said, according to their opinions. He had begun to think like them, and was now looking forward to a life, a happy life, like other married people he had seen, and the comforts and joys that came with it. But to face it, and to go through the procedures of achieving it, was awkward, and the future, if the marriage was agreed, was bleak because of his accommodation problem and his financial situation. Throughout the journey his mind was full of these thoughts, all mixed up. It seemed everything in the future was dark. The only brightness he could visualise was the beautiful smiling face of a young woman he had not seen yet, and the innocent face of a little girl who might call him father, even though he was not her father. And the prospect of walking on the road with those two, knowing that he would be their protector.

An old man came hurrying from the house on to the verandah, followed by a little girl and an old woman with a veil completely covering her body.

'Salaam alaykum!' the old man said with a broad smile on his face, throwing both hands in the air and walking towards the truck. Mustafa opened the door of the truck, and everyone inside said: 'Wa-alaykum is-salaam.' Mustafa got out of the truck and shook hands with the old man and embraced him, kissed him on both cheeks, and hugged him again affectionately. The old woman said: 'Salaam alaykum,' and everyone returned the greeting.

Sayeed got out and held the door for Halima. The two women went towards the old woman and embraced her.

'That's my brother, Sayeed,' Mustafa said.

Sayeed smiled.

'Kayf haalak?' the old man asked.

'Al-hamdulillah, shukran,' Sayeed replied.

The old couple looked at Sayeed for a few seconds, checking him from head to toe, and trying to keep the same friendly smile on their faces. But Sayeed's skinny, fragile figure was disappointing and the old man struggled not to let his expression change just in case others would notice any rejection of Sayeed.

'Welcome, welcome. Please come inside,' the old man said, bowing his head towards Sayeed and Mustafa.

Mustafa closed the doors of his truck, and started

walking towards the verandah of the bungalow. The old man and Sayeed walked on either side of him, and the women followed.

'I think we will let the ladies go in and talk to Latifa, and we will sit on the verandah. Is that all right?' the old man asked.

'Yes, yes. It's fine. It is a bit cooler here,' Mustafa said.

'Please ask Latifa to bring some *gahwa*,' the old man said to his wife. The woman shook her head and went in with the other women. The men sat on the verandah, and the little girl went slowly and sat on the old man's lap.

The square front yard with its white sand was covered with the lengthening shadows of date palm trees. The truck was standing in the middle of the yard facing the verandah. Beyond the sandy yard, and all around the bungalow, were the tall date palm trees with their wide leaves. The three men were sitting cross-legged, quietly, looking at the front yard. The little girl, with her long double-pleated hair combed neatly and tied with little red ribbons, was wearing a blue floral dress that came down to her ankles. She was sitting still on the old man's lap, her head resting on one of his thighs, and her two stubby bare feet dangling over his other side. She was sucking her right thumb, twisting the old man's white beard with the little fingers of her left hand.

'I knew your father,' the old man said. 'Yes, he was a good man, a kind man too. Everyone liked him. After your mother died, he changed so fast and aged so quickly,' he said, stroking the little girl's hair which was slightly wet with sweat. He was rocking slightly, forwards and backwards. Mustafa and Sayeed were silent, looking at the wizened face of the old man.

'You were both little then. It was a hard time. Food was scarce, and money was too. But we lived, though not in such luxury as nowadays. You can buy anything now, all the strange goods from foreign lands, but in the old days we were hungry. Youngsters these days do not understand what hardship is. They never will.'

'We knew the hardship, uncle, and we still know it,' Mustafa said.

'Still, not a very long time to go for me,' the old man said with a sigh.

'No, no, don't speak like that. You are still quite young and strong and probably you will outlive both of us,' Mustafa said.

'I would like to think that I will live for many years,' the old man said, raising his eyebrows and wrinkling his forehead. 'But let us be realistic. I do not think I will see this child get married,' he said, adjusting the head of the little girl who was already fast asleep. The movement caused the child to push in the thumb which was already falling from her slightly open mouth. He patted the child's hip gently with his left hand.

'This is a lovely child. She is attached to me so much. She sleeps with me, and follows me around from morning till evening, poor thing. She cannot go to sleep without sucking her thumb, and she must twist my beard with the other hand at the same time. I don't understand it. My wife is old too, and we want to find a kind person for this child's mother before we pass away,' the old man said, looking at Sayeed. Sayeed looked at Mustafa and lowered his eyes. The old man glanced outside, and Sayeed saw the old man's moist eyes, and the sadness in his withered face. Mustafa cleared his throat, stretched his legs, and asked how old the little girl was.

'She is only two years old, bless the little one. I wish her father was alive today. You know how he died, don't you?'

'Yes, yes. I heard he was involved in an accident,' Mustafa said.

'He used to collect vegetables from the farms in the village, and take them to the city. One day when he was driving back, a big water tanker collided with his truck, and that was the end. Life can end so quickly, and that changes others' lives completely, in a split second. My daughter is still young, and we do not want to leave her on her own when we go. She is a beautiful girl,' the old man said. Mustafa looked at Sayeed and shook his head.

'They have taken a long time making that *gahwa*, haven't they?' the old man said in a loud voice, turning towards the door so that the women would hear him.

'That's the problem with women. When they get together, they have a lot to talk about. Most of the time it is either rubbish, or gossip,' the old man said, and they all laughed.

Chapter 10

There were no shadows on the yard now, only the white sand reflecting the dusk and the silhouetted figure of the truck with its shiny chrome-plated front grille and head lamps.

A rustle of dresses and a giggling noise were heard. All the women came out on to the verandah, one by one, in their black veils. First the old woman, followed by Halima, Akila, and the bride-to-be. They all carried something. The old woman had a plate of cakes, Halima a plate of ripe dates, Akila a tray full of small handleless white china cups, and Latifa a brass coffee pot containing *gahwa*, the cardamom coffee. Just visible through their veils, the women's smiling faces were covered with glistening drops of sweat, illuminated by the dusk as they came silently on to the verandah. The women put everything they had brought in front of the men, and withdrew slowly inside. Then a burst of laughter was heard from inside, someone said: 'Shh . . .' and all went quiet.

Sayeed looked at Mustafa. He was grinning widely. The old man was happy, and he cleared his throat and said: 'Let's have some coffee.'

Mustafa pushed the tray towards the old man who adjusted the palm fibre filter inside the curved nozzle of the brass coffee pot, and poured the cardamom coffee into three small cups, lifting the pot well above them. A curve of liquid from the nozzle fell into the cups and filled them with fragrant light brown *gahwa*. He gave two cups to the brothers, said a prayer and took a small sip, swallowed it, and put the cup back in front of them. The two brothers sipped their coffee.

'It's nice coffee,' Mustafa said.

'Yes. It's very nice,' Sayeed said.

'Please eat some of these cakes. Latifa made them especially for you,' the old man said, and he passed the tray of cakes towards Sayeed and Mustafa.

The little girl woke up, and sat with her eyes wide open, curled up against the old man's chest, her head tucked just below his chin. She started sucking her thumb while stroking his beard, watching the visitors. Sayeed took some dates and started eating them.

'While you are drinking coffee, let me go inside and ask my wife something,' the old man said, and he started to walk inside with the little girl following him. On his way, he switched on the fluorescent light on the verandah.

The brothers were quiet. Occasionally they ate a date and sipped coffee. The verandah, and a small part of the yard were bathed in white light. The date palm grove beyond it was in total darkness. Flying insects were coming in, and some of them were flying towards the light, hitting the fluorescent tube, making a dull hollow noise and falling down, while others were circling around it. Now and then, some of the insects on their way towards the light would hit the faces of the brothers who were sitting pensively on the mat, drinking their

94

coffee and munching the dates. They slapped their faces and necks whenever an insect hit them.

'I hope they do not ask us to stay for supper,' Sayeed said.

'I hope they do! I like to taste another woman's cooking. They all cook differently, you know, and the food always tastes different too.'

'It is quite late now. Also, I have to leave for the city tomorrow.'

'Tomorrow! Why so early? You could stay for a few more days. Village life is good for you. City kills people young.'

'The day after tomorrow I have to go back to work.'

'You could sleep late tomorrow morning.'

The old man came back on to the verandah, screwed his eyes against the fluorescent light and put his cupped hand over them to look at the two brothers sitting on the mat.

'It has got dark quickly, hasn't it?' he said, still holding his hand over his eyes and looking outside.

'Some more coffee?' the old man asked, sitting down in front of the brothers.

'No thank you, uncle, we are fine,' Mustafa said.

Everyone was quiet for a few seconds, and the old man glanced at the brothers, looked down and started stroking the curved handle of the coffee pot.

'All right then, let us talk business, shall we?' the old man said. 'I spoke to my wife and daughter. Your wife Akila knows my daughter. We know your family, and Latifa seems to like you, Sayeed,' he said, moving his hand towards Sayeed, and then withdrawing it slowly, and starting to adjust his *gutra*.

'So, what do you think?' he asked.

95

Mustafa stared at Sayeed who was sitting cross-legged, looking down at the mat and scraping it with the nail of his forefinger.

'What do you think, Sayeed?' Mustafa asked in a deep voice. 'Would you like to marry her, Sayeed?' Mustafa bent forward, and tilted his head sideways to look into Sayeed's face. Sayeed did not say anything. He was looking down, running his forefinger over the elevated ridges of the plastic mat. Mustafa repeated the question.

'Hmm . . .' Sayeed said, without raising his head.

Mustafa burst out laughing, and the old man joined him.

'He is a little shy, this brother of mine. Please excuse him, uncle,' Mustafa said, adjusting his *gutra*, and stretching his legs, his body shaking with laughter.

'Have some more coffee?' the old man said.

'Well, just a little then,' Mustafa said.

The old man poured some coffee into their cups, and started to stroke his beard. 'My wife and I have decided to ask for a dowry of twenty-five thousand dinars. Latifa also needs some gold jewellery, and new furniture for her home,' the old man said slowly, pausing every few words for emphasis. Sayeed and Mustafa looked at each other, and then looked at the old man. He kept a serious face, and was looking at them with firmness in his eyes, stroking his moustache and beard.

After a few seconds, which seemed like a long time to everyone, Mustafa said: 'Uncle, Sayeed does not earn a lot of money. You know we are not rich people.'

'How is he going to manage a family then?' the old man asked quickly.

'His salary is not too bad, but he has not been working

that long, and then the furniture, and jewellery, that amounts to a lot. Please let us be a bit more realistic.'

'I am sorry. I cannot have a dowry less than twenty-five thousand dinars for my daughter, and the furniture and the jewellery is for the new family, anyway,' the old man said.

'I know, I know, but weddings are expensive. We need money for the wedding ceremony as well. Please be a little more understanding.'

Sayeed was quiet, looking at the faces of the old man and Mustafa in turn. The old man was sitting still, cross-legged, very erect, his firm eyes fixed on the brothers.

'My daughter is young, and she is beautiful. I am sure we can find her a good husband who can afford a reasonable dowry of twenty-five thousand dinars. It is not too much! In our village, as you know, the average dowry for a beautiful young girl is about forty thousand dinars.'

'But uncle . . .' Mustafa said, moving both his cupped hands slowly towards the old man, then withdrawing. He stopped what he was going to say, and looked at Sayeed's face. 'But uncle . . .' he began again. 'Latifa was married before. I am sorry to say this, but she has a child too.'

'She was married. We all know that,' the old man said, moving his body in an agitated way. He looked at both brothers, then towards the door of the house.

'The child, I want to keep her here, if Latifa will allow us to have her. She does not cost anything to feed, poor little lamb,' the old man said, and his body sagged.

'Can you afford twenty thousand dinars then?'

'Can you go down a little bit more, uncle? The

jewellery alone will cost at least another fifteen thousand dinars.'

'No, no more,' the old man said, shaking his head sideways. This the brothers understood to be the final sum.

'If that's what you must have, you must have it. We might have to sell some animals to raise the money for all these expenses, but my brother must settle down, and your daughter is a good woman, everyone says. He is a lucky man, uncle, if he can marry her.'

'What about the jewellery for her, and the furniture for the house?'

'Let her select those, and you can tell us how much they cost. Then we can see to the money. I suppose we don't have any choice in the things she selects,' Mustafa asked.

'She will not be extravagant. It will be the minimum expense, I can assure you. We are not rich people, so don't worry about that,' the old man said. 'So, do we agree to this?'

'Yes, I think so,' Mustafa said, and he looked at Sayeed.

'Yes. Yes. That is fine,' Sayeed said, and the old man shook hands with both brothers, and confirmed the betrothal.

'Let us talk about something different now,' the old man suggested, wiping the sweat off his forehead with his *gutra*. 'They have cooked some nice camel meat, and chicken too. Please stay and have something to eat before you go. Is that all right?'

'It is very kind of you, uncle, but isn't it too much trouble?' Mustafa asked.

'No, no, young man, we are very hospitable people.

We don't let our visitors go without letting them eat something first. In fact, the ladies are getting the meal ready now.'

Sayeed was sitting quietly, hands clasped on his lap.

'Sayeed . . .' the old man said, looking into Sayeed's eyes. 'Please look after my daughter.'

'Yes, uncle, I will,' Sayeed promised quietly.

'You know, uncle, he wants to take the bride to the city, where he works,' Mustafa said.

'I thought that might happen. After all, you work there. The city is all right for young people, but I do not like it; it is always busy. I like the peaceful life of the village. Latifa grew up in the village, but she is young, and she will like it, I am sure. I hope she will leave the child here, but if she takes her, I am sure she will be sent to a good school there. Our village school is not good. I read in the newspapers that a lot of girls go to school now, and most of them work too. Some become doctors, and there are women teachers now. It is like in foreign countries. Changes are coming. It may be for the good.'

'With respect, uncle, you don't seem to know much about the city. Life there is very difficult. Goods are expensive. It is very crowded, and you are no one there, you will always be an outsider. For girls, if they learn to read and write, that should be enough,' Mustafa said.

'At my age, I do not think too much about the decisions our next generation is going to make, for the simple reason that they will do whatever they want, whether you like it or not. I may think they are on a destructive path, but it does not happen that way. Every new generation will be different from the previous one; that is the beauty of life, and change does not mean destruction. In the end, they will lead a life like anyone else, living anywhere else.'

The old woman appeared at the door, and cleared her throat.

'Yes?' the old man asked.

'The meal is ready. Do you want to come inside and eat it, or would you prefer to eat it out here?'

'What do you think?' the old man asked the brothers.

'It is cooler here. Why don't we eat out here, and the ladies can eat inside the house,' Mustafa said.

'All right then. I will bring your food here,' she said, and turned around to go in.

'We have agreed on the marriage, and we are going to have a wedding soon,' the old man announced with a smile on his face. The old woman turned around, and whispered a prayer with her eyes looking upwards. Then she looked at the old man and said, 'I am glad,' and she leaned against the door frame, and looked at everyone. They were all silent. She raised the edge of her *abaya*, and wiped the tears from the corner of her eyes.

'We will talk about it later. Now, let us eat something,' the old man said, slapping both hands on his thighs.

They ate well, and talked loudly about the old times, hard times, and happy times. Already they were feeling part of one family. The women were happy too. Halima mentioned the children several times, and said that they ought to be going home soon, and she was surprised at how excited Akila was. Latifa did not say much. She was feeding the child, who was falling asleep by this time.

It was late, and everyone was feeling tired as they prepared to leave. The old couple were happy, and relieved. At the same time, a great sadness engulfed them when they thought of their daughter leaving home to go to the city. They were anxious too, when they thought about their granddaughter; wondering whether her future stepfather would treat her well, and look after her properly. Sayeed seemed a quiet, kind, gentle person. They could not imagine any harm would come to their granddaughter.

The date was set for the wedding, and Akila offered to help Latifa sew her trousseau.

They all agreed to meet again soon to discuss the details, and Mustafa thanked the old man, his wife, and Latifa for their kindness, and for the excellent meal. Then they got into the truck and left for home.

On the way back, everyone was quiet. The bright head lamps of the truck illuminated the tracks, and the date palm trees on either side, as Mustafa drove slowly on the narrow tracks.

'I think it went very well,' Mustafa said.

'You'd better be careful what you are saying, it's been too much for him already. Poor Sayeed didn't expect any of this. It must be a shock for him,' Halima said.

'Ahk. He is all right. I know him,' Mustafa said.

The little illumination from the dashboard, and the reflected light from outside, lit up the faces of the four sitting inside the truck.

'I made a small poem for our brother Sayeed,' Akila said.

'Please keep it to yourself. This woman. She makes up rubbish poems, and I think she is mad,' Mustafa laughed.

'The desert rose looks rough and lifeless

In the dry hostile sand.
But in the early misty morning
With the dew drops glistening on its petals
It looks more beautiful
Than any rose on land.'

Chapter 11

It was after midnight when they got back home. As soon as Mustafa stopped the truck, Sayeed opened the door and got out, followed by Halima and Akila. Sayeed shut the door, and Mustafa drove the truck to the parking place in the back garden. It was dark on the verandah and in the front garden. The women walked slowly, holding up their skirts and watching their feet. Sayeed followed them. Halima climbed up the steps on to the verandah and switched on the fluorescent light which fired hesitantly several times, and lit finally. Akila rushed inside, followed by Halima. Sayeed stood on the verandah, stretched his hands above him and yawned.

The two older children were sitting on a mat in the sitting-room playing draughts. The rest were asleep in the same room. The children who were playing draughts turned their heads to look at the women and turned their heads back and carried on playing. Akila went towards her sleeping child. She pulled the little girl's dress down, and straightened her head. The child did not wake, but turned on her right side and put her palm under her cheek.

The desert cooler was blowing cold humid air, and making a rattling, humming noise.

'Hope they've eaten something,' Halima said.

'Don't wake them up now, let them sleep,' Akila said, getting up and taking her *abaya* off.

'Some of these children didn't eat much at lunch time.'

'But don't wake them up. They will not eat, even if you wake them. I am taking my daughter upstairs.' Akila picked up her little girl and carried her upstairs. Halima took her *abaya* off and dropped it on the floor. She looked at the children, sighed, and went to the kitchen to make the cup of tea which she had missed so badly.

Mustafa came in through the kitchen and looked at the boys playing draughts, and told them to stop and go to sleep. Sayeed went on to the verandah and sat on the floor with his back against the wall. He was still deep in thought. Excitement about the young woman was still in the back of his mind, but other serious thoughts of how he was going to find the money for the dowry, jewellery, and other expenses also crowded in. Mustafa might help a little, but he was poor. Sayeed's savings would cover some of the costs, but the big dowry, and the jewellery, were a problem. Abdul Mubarak was his only hope, he thought. He must ask him for a loan. He was sure that Abdul Mubarak would give him one. Even though he was a devilish person, he could be kind too. His good personality and his evil one existed so closely together: no one knew when one would change to the other.

The children collected the draughts in their cupped hands, and dropped them into an empty dried milk tin. The rattle woke up one of the little children who was sleeping on the mat. She started crying. Halima went rushing to her, picked the little girl up, and asked whether she would like to eat something. The child shook her head, but Halima carried her to the kitchen, the little girl's cheek resting on her shoulder, and tried to feed her with some leftovers from lunch. But the girl refused, and kept shaking her head. Halima was persistent. The child was forced to accept a spoonful, and went to sleep with her mouth slightly open and some food falling out of it, on to Halima's shoulder. This made Halima very angry, but she was helpless. She did not want to hit her in case the girl started crying again. She took the child back to the sitting-room, and put her on the mat where the two boys who had been playing draughts earlier were now sleeping.

Akila came downstairs, wearing a different dress. She looked at Halima who was sitting on the floor near the sleeping children.

'I wouldn't mind some tea as well,' Akila said.

Halima took a sip of tea from a cup, swallowed it, gave a big sigh, and said, 'These children have not eaten anything.'

'Oh, don't worry about it too much, Halima. They will be hungry by tomorrow morning, and will eat twice as much. I will ask the men whether they would like tea as well,' Akila said, and went on to the verandah where Mustafa and Sayeed were sitting.

'Would you like some tea?'

'Yes,' they said.

'Perhaps we should discuss the marriage tonight, because our brother has to go back tomorrow,' Akila said.

Halima came and sat on the verandah, and Akila made some tea, served the men, then sat next to Halima.

'You could ask the Yemeni tailor in the village to make two *thorbe*s for our brother,' Halima said.

'Yes, I will do that. Perhaps one silk one and one cotton one,' Mustafa said.

'I don't like the silk ones. They are transparent,' Sayeed said.

'Ah, don't worry about that. It looks much better than a cotton *thorbe*,' Mustafa said.

'We all have to have new dresses,' Halima added.

'That will cost a lot of money,' Mustafa said.

'I can bring some dresses for the children from the city,' Sayeed said.

'You don't know what to select,' Halima said.

'Never mind, brother, it is not easy to select dresses for children. We can easily do that down here,' Akila offered.

'Don't worry too much about the wedding. We will do it as simply as we can. We still have to gather some money for the dowry, jewellery, and furniture. I might have to ask some of my friends at the hospital for a loan,' Sayeed said.

'We should not have agreed to such a high dowry,' Mustafa said.

'Don't talk about it now. It's agreed and we have to honour it. If you give me the money, I will go with Latifa to buy her jewellery,' Akila said.

'I didn't bring a lot of money with me,' Sayeed said.

'Where do you keep your money?' Mustafa asked.

'I have left it with a friend of mine.'

'Can you trust him?'

'Of course! He is an honest boy,' Sayeed said. 'And I am thinking of asking a friend at work for a loan,' Sayeed said again.

'I don't think that's a good idea,' Mustafa warned.

'What else can I do? He is a good man, Abdul

Mubarak. He will lend me some money. If not, I could ask Mohammed Sofail. He is richer than all of them. His father owns a wholesale grocery shop. He has lots of money, and he is a very religious person. This is funny. His brother went and bought a television set, and Sofail smashed it, saying it was against his religion, and it could corrupt people.'

'Then what did his brother do?' Mustafa asked.

'He went and bought another set, and threatened to kill Sofail if he touched it.'

Everyone laughed.

'Did Sofail break that too?' Halima asked.

'No. He did not touch it. He is a very religious man, but I do not like him very much, because he is too strict,' Sayeed said. 'Look! Don't worry too much about the wedding clothes for me. In the city they are so cheap, and the *thorbe*s come ready made, from China. All different sizes, and folded nicely in clear plastic bags. I am wearing one of them now. Very cheap,' Sayeed said.

'This is your wedding, and you must wear good clothes. Let that Yemeni in the village make your *thorbe* for you. Tomorrow, before you go back to the city, I will take you to him. He can take the necessary measurements, and it will be ready by the time you come again,' Mustafa insisted.

'All right then. But I don't want any silk ones.'

'They are nice, brother. Just have one of them made, for the wedding day, and do not fuss,' Akila said in a soft voice.

'Don't make a fuss, Sayeed. We have a lot of things to do. Get the clothes made here, and get a silk one as well, and just send us the money for the expenses,' Halima said firmly.

'How am I going to send the money?'

'I think the best thing would be for you to come here again before the wedding, with the money, and we can settle everything beforehand. Then you could come back, get married, and take your bride to the city,' Mustafa suggested.

'That's a good idea, but I will have to do something about my hut first. Either I will have to get another hut, or get some friends to make my hut bigger, because I like the area where I live. The people are not bad, nor are the children, and it is not too noisy,' Sayeed said.

'Do what you have to do, but do it quickly before the woman changes her mind,' Mustafa said, and he gave a loud laugh.

'I think it is getting late. I am going to bed,' Halima said.

'I feel sleepy too,' said Akila.

'Don't keep her waiting too long,' Halima said, bending towards Mustafa, and then walking hurriedly inside the house.

'Every chance she gets, she wants to be nasty,' Akila said, shaking her head and looking at Mustafa and Sayeed. They did not say anything. Mustafa started to whistle slowly, and Sayeed cleared his throat.

After the women had gone to bed, Mustafa pretended to be sleepy. He got up and asked Sayeed to lock the front door before he went to bed.

Sayeed sat on the verandah, watching the flying insects circle the fluorescent light. Everyone else in the house was sleeping now. It seemed the whole world was sleeping, and he was the only one awake, left with newly acquired problems to sort out. It had taken a few years for him to settle down, and he had got into the routine of his single, care-free life, but now it seemed all that was finished, and he had to start again. A latent longing had erupted strangely, with a new desire for change, and he felt grateful in a way to his family for arranging this. It, like his youth, had come back after a long absence, to make him happy.

All his savings would be used up, and he still needed more money. That he would have to borrow from friends if possible. If they could not lend it, he did not know what he would do. He was sure that they would all laugh at the thought of him getting married, but he did not care any more. The woman was young, and perhaps he would do better than all his friends.

Sayeed felt very sleepy. He stood up, switched the light off, lay down on the mat on the verandah, and went to sleep.

Chapter 12

Sayeed was woken up by the crowing and clucking of poultry, and the rustling, screeching birds in the date palm grove. It had been a cold night, the sky was getting lighter now, and the bushes in the front garden, and the houses on the skyline on the other side of the valley, were beginning to appear. A distant prayer call with its mystic, rhythmic echo made him feel serene and relaxed. He closed his eyes, and repeated the prayer call silently.

He noticed some activity in the kitchen, and heard Halima trying to wake up the boys for the early morning prayer. He got up, collected his *gutra*, put his slippers on, went out to the garden, and walked towards the pump. The two older boys came out through the back door, sleepy and silent. They washed quickly, and went back inside through the kitchen. Sayeed had his wash slowly and went back to the verandah and prayed on his own.

The children were noisy at breakfast, the younger ones making a fuss about the food, and the older ones eating fast and bullying the little ones. Halima, who had been up early in the morning preparing the breakfast, looked exhausted. Akila looked happy and relaxed.

Mustafa and Sayeed finished their breakfast, and went on to the verandah. Mustafa lit a cigarette, sat down in his place near the wall, and Sayeed took his toothbrush stick, and started to clean his teeth.

'I think I ought to be going soon,' Sayeed said.

'Well, I will take you to the main road in the pick-up, there are plenty of vehicles on that road going to the city. Those open trucks are cheap.'

'But they are very bumpy and you get covered with dust. You could get thrown out as well,' Sayeed said.

'Not if you hold on to the sides firmly. The floor is a bit hard, but they usually have a foam mattress on it.'

'I am not going in one of those! I want to get to the city in one piece, and if I get injured I will not be able to work for a while. No work means no money.'

'Please yourself, You have to pay almost double for those minibuses. Anyway, I will take you to the Yemeni tailor in the village to be measured for your *thorbe*s on our way to the main road.'

Sayeed found it difficult to say goodbye to everyone, especially to Halima who did not say much about the wedding plans, but reminded him that he should come back to the village soon with some money so that they could buy the jewellery and other essentials for the wedding. Akila looked sad. She was carrying her little girl on her hip, and wiped her eyes with the back of her hand. Sayeed took his bundle of clothes, and got into the truck where Mustafa was waiting. Sayeed waved to the women and children, as the engine started revving fast. Mustafa took the hand brake off, and the truck started to move forward towards the valley.

'Don't look back,' Mustafa said.

'Why?'

'Never look back. It only makes a man feel bad.

Always look straight ahead, and keep looking ahead until you know that they cannot see you. Keep going until you know that goodbye was something in the past,' Mustafa said.

'You are a hard man,' Sayeed said, and he put his hand out and waved to the women and children who were standing in the front yard.

'Ahk. That's the trouble with you. Too soft.'

He pressed the horn several times, and started to laugh, his whole body shaking.

'As soon as you have married your woman, you must think of getting another one.'

'I think your jokes are vile, Mustafa. You must not forget that I am older than you,' Sayeed said.

Mustafa went quiet, and took his packet of cigarettes out of his breast pocket, and lit one, with both his hands off the steering-wheel.

'We are not far from the tailor's shop,' Mustafa said, putting his hands back on the steering-wheel, puffing out some smoke from the side of his mouth while he spoke, the cigarette wedged in the other corner of his mouth.

'That is the shop. I hope he is awake.'

'Yes. The shutters are up, so it must be open,' Sayeed said. Mustafa stopped the truck in front of the tailor's shop, close to the front steps, and looked through the aluminium-framed, clear glass front door of the shop, which was a flat-roofed building on an elevated bank by the road. Inside some finished garments were hanging in a tall glass case with a bright fluorescent light inside. Some water was leaking from the desert cooler which was fixed to the outside wall. Small stalactites were hanging underneath the cooler. The Yemeni tailor was sitting behind a sewing-machine, a few feet inside the front door, with his kilt pulled above the knee. When Sayeed and Mustafa walked in, he got up and greeted them.

'Salaam alaykum,' the Yemeni said.

'Wa-alaykum is-salaam,' Mustafa replied, and shook hands with him.

'This is my brother, Sayeed. I do not know whether you know him.'

'Yes. Yes. I know him. He left for the city just after I came to the village,' the Yemeni said.

'Well, he is in a hurry to go back to the city today. He is going to get married soon, and we want the best *thorbe*s you can make,' Mustafa said.

'I will try my best,' the Yemeni answered. 'Do you have any material?' he asked.

'No, we were hoping to buy some cloth from you. Do you have any good material?'

'Yes, I have some bales of cloth. You select the cloth, and I will take the measurements. It will be ready in a week.'

'We want two *thorbe*s, one silk and one cotton,' Mustafa said.

'White silk or yellow silk?'

'White is better. Don't you think so, Sayeed?'

'Yes,' said Sayeed.

The Yemeni took the measurements, and Sayeed gave him a deposit. Mustafa thanked the Yemeni, left the shop, got back in the truck, and started driving towards the main road.

The metallic rattle of the truck, and the dull thump of the wheels on the dust track broke the silence. From the valley, it was a difficult climb to the tarred road, over a rough rocky track which could slash tyres like sharp knives.

They came to the road, near a bridge over the valley. The dusty wheels of the truck made imprints on the melting tar. The road ran uphill to the left and vanished. The fossilised stumps of trees that had lived on this land long ago were scattered on the barren brown earth with ammonites and other remains of the marine life that had once flourished here.

'On the other side of the mountain, they have built a new road. It is very dangerous. Many fast vehicles travel on it. But it takes you to the city quickly,' Mustafa said.

'I got off at that bridge when I came,' Sayeed said.

'Yes, but if you stay here, you might have to stay for a long time. Up near the main road you could catch a lift quickly,' Mustafa said.

'We will see,' Sayeed said, wiping the sweat off his face with his *gutra*. 'Why don't you get your air-conditioner fixed?'

'Ahk, it's all right. I think it needs a bit of freon. I must take it to the Yemeni garage one of these days,' Mustafa replied.

'Is there another Yemeni in the village?'

'Oh, yes. There are quite a few now. There used to be none, but now there is a garage with Yemeni workers, a car battery place with Yemeni workers, and that tailor's shop. One of the grocery shops has some Yemeni workers as well. They don't own the shops. Our people own them. The Yemenis only work there, and our people get most of the income. It is a lazy way to earn money. But the Yemenis are quite happy doing those jobs, so why worry? They take a lot of money home when they go back to see their families, once every two years or so. A little money here is a lot in their country. They are very hard workers. They look small, but they are very strong,' Mustafa told him.

'Yes, I have seen them in the city carrying huge refrigerators on their backs,' Sayeed said.

'Ah, there it is, the road to the city,' Mustafa said, pointing to the road about a mile away, below the hill on which they were travelling until the turning on the slope, which led to the main road.

'Koreans made that road,' Mustafa said.

Sayeed shook his head.

'Yes. Very hard workers, and lots of big machines, and they finished it very quickly as well. All yellow machines, their buses were yellow as well. They flattened the earth. Sometimes they had to flatten the hills too, but they were quick. Could you have imagined a road like that, a few years ago? Now these foreigners are brought in, they work for us, and it is good for our country.'

Sayeed did not say anything. They were getting closer to the main road. The fast-moving Mercedes lorries with their huge wheels and massive engines, the drivers sitting very high up in their cabs, their *gutra*s moving in the wind, all the coloured decorations and the bulbs inside and out, the red fibre carpets on the dashboard, on the floors, on the seats, the Arabic music and the constant blowing of the horns, all this reminded him of the city. Japanese and American cars travelled fast in both directions. They would overtake other vehicles even when there was something coming on the other side, and one would have to go up on to the kerb to avoid a collision. The main road ran at right angles to the small road on which Sayeed and Mustafa were driving. Their truck came to the crossroads. Mustafa stopped close to the main road, which was on a slight elevation. The noise of the vehicles on the road was so loud, they had to shout at each other to be heard.

'Now, don't be bashful, Sayeed. Change your behaviour a bit. Soon you will have to look after a woman and a child. Otherwise they will have to look after you,' Mustafa said with a smile.

'I am not bashful, and don't worry about me. I am sure, God willing, everything will be all right,' Sayeed said.

'I talk too much sometimes, but please don't be angry. You know I mean well,' Mustafa said.

'Ahk, forget it, Mustafa. You can tell me anything. I don't mind,' Sayeed said, opening his door.

'Well, the best thing to do is to stand near the road, and signal for a vehicle to stop,' Mustafa said.

Sayeed wiped his face with the *gutra*, and covered his nose with it.

'I will stay here until you get a lift. Drink some water first, and take these two cans of Pepsi with you,' Mustafa said, getting out of the truck himself. Sayeed drank some water from the plastic container on the floor, gathered his bundle, put the two cans of Pepsi in his pocket and got out of the truck. Outside, it was extremely hot. After a while, Sayeed and Mustafa managed to stop a Toyota minibus. There were a few passengers already on it. Sayeed agreed to the fare, got on to the bus, put his bundle on a seat, and waved to Mustafa. The bus started to move as Sayeed sat down.

Chapter 13

It was late afternoon, the sun was going down and the air was turning cooler. It had been a long, weary journey. The minibus was full now. Sayeed had tried to sleep, but the constant shaking of the bus and the noise of the cassette player were too distracting. Everyone in the minibus was tired. Sayeed felt a great loneliness. He thought of the events of the last two days. So many unexpected things had happened. He had gone to the village because Mustafa had sent him a letter asking him to come. It had been a long time since he left the village, and he had wanted to see his family. He was hoping to go back soon as he did not request many days off. Now, something completely unexpected was about to happen, and there were busy weeks ahead. He felt anxious when he thought about the extra money he had to find. He felt nervous about his future life, the woman and child who might not settle down in the city. So many thoughts were crossing his weary mind, but he felt sure that he would get the backing of his family, and even of his friends who worked with him in the hospital.

The city started appearing on the horizon. Although the sun had gone down, the sky was still red and the faraway buildings were silhouetted against it. Scattered illuminations and dotted sodium street lights started to appear in the distance. Head lamp beams filtered through the dust clouds which blew on the desert tracks parallel to the main road. Some drivers left the main road and drove on the tracks on either side of it to avoid the traffic jams on the way into the city. On the outskirts of the city, scattered huts and small mud houses started to appear, and herds of black goats led by women and children. Closer to the city, rows of busy shops with bright pink and green fluorescent lights sprang up on either side of the road. Music came blaring out of small restaurants. Some of them had chicken grills outside, with ten to twenty whole chickens revolving on metal skewers, roasting in tall ovens fed by the propane cylinders that stood beside them. Waiters were serving customers: flat peta bread and whole chicken thrown on to paper, with pickles and green chillies, wrapped up well, and eaten hot. Sayeed felt hungry. He would have to eat some chicken as soon as he arrived at the bus station, before he went back to his hut. The traffic was moving slowly around the carpet *souk*. Fluorescent tubes hanging on wires tied to date palm trees illuminated the area. The road near the *souk* had worn away, and was full of pot holes, slowing down the traffic. The carpets looked bright in the dusky light.

They were in the city at last, the streets lit with bright street lamps. Now the traffic was moving fast again, and it did not take long for them to reach the bus terminal. The passengers got ready to leave as the bus drew up.

Sayeed was the last to get off. He took his bundle of clothes and walked towards a cafeteria. The smell of food was in the air. Sayeed saw kebab stands, with gas fires to cook the cylinders of camel meat, and omelettes frying on flat metal plates. There were clay pots with narrow necks simmering over flames, and a man stirring the sticky meaty mixture inside with a long-handled spoon. There was the smell of oven-baking fresh flat bread. The whole area was bathed in fluorescent light. Sayeed was going into the cafeteria when the Egyptian waiter asked him what he wanted. Sayeed said he wanted some chicken and bread, and would eat it inside. The Egyptian asked him to take a seat, and he brought an aluminium jug of water and a tumbler, and put them on a plastic-covered table. He asked Sayeed whether he would like a drink of tea or coffee.

The Egyptian went to the chicken oven outside, opened its sliding doors, and took out one of the long metal skewers and pushed the meat off on to a plate, put back the skewer with the rest of the chickens, in the oven, and shut the doors.

A whole chicken on a plate, and some peta bread next to it, with a bowl of pickled cucumbers, aubergines, and olives, some fresh green chillies, raw sliced onions and houmous were placed in small dishes before Sayeed.

Sayeed took a sip from a glass of hot sweet tea, put it down, shook the tea bag up and down several times, and put it in the ash tray. He bit off a piece of chicken leg, and started to eat it slowly. The cafeteria was crowded.

Sayeed was wondering whether to catch another bus to his hut, or to walk up to the hospital to see Hameed, and ask him whether he could stay in the laboratory that night. He was exhausted, but he wanted to tell his story to everyone, even to the people in the cafeteria. Probably it will be Hameed first, he thought.

He paid the man at the cafeteria, and started to walk towards the hospital. The wide road was crowded with traffic. The new date palm trees planted in the islands in the middle of the dual carriageway were still. The grass around the trees on these islands was scanty, most of it was dried up. Sayeed walked towards the hospital with his bundle over his shoulder.

The guard at the entrance recognised Sayeed, and after exchanging greetings, he asked Sayeed what he was doing there at that time of the night. Sayeed said he was on his way to see his friend Hameed in the laboratory, and he added that Hameed stayed in the laboratory to look after the place. The guard let Sayeed go through.

The laboratory doors were closed, but he knew that the side door was not locked. All the lights were on in every room, but he could not see anyone. Sayeed went into the sitting-room and found Hameed sleeping in a chair in the corner. The black-and-white television set was on the table in the middle of the room, tuned to the only channel available. Sayeed cleared his throat, and looked at Hameed, but he was still sleeping. So he put his bundle on the table and went to the toilet next to the biochemistry department.

When he came back, Hameed was sitting up in his chair, rubbing his eyes.

'Ah, Sayeed, salaam alaykum,' Hameed said.

'Wa-alaykum is-salaam,' Sayeed said with a smile, sitting down next to Hameed.

'When did you get back?'

'Today. This evening. I haven't been back to my place yet. I thought I would come and see you first,' Sayeed said.

'How is your family?'

'Fine.'

'Your brother?'

'All right.'

'And his children?'

'All fine.'

'You came back so soon?'

'I didn't have many days off.'

'That's bad, especially when you had to go that far.'

'That's life. But some unexpected things happened too.'

'What's that?'

'Nothing much.'

'Please tell me. Is it something good or bad?'

'Well, I don't know,' Sayeed said, leaning forward in his chair and rubbing his hands together.

'Let us have some tea, Sayeed, and then perhaps you will tell me about it,' Hameed said, getting up.

'They want me to get married.'

'What?' Hameed exclaimed, and he started laughing. 'That is very good. I mustn't laugh. My family are also pestering me to get married, and I know how they can be,' Hameed said.

'It's all arranged now.'

'So soon? Did they arrange everything before you went there?'

'It seems so. I was very annoyed at first, but they all thought it was a good idea, and I am beginning to think it is good. I am getting old, and I will have no one to look after me if I stay too long unmarried.'

'I think it is a good idea too. God willing, you will be all right,' Hameed said with a serious face. 'So, when is it going to be?'

'We don't know yet. Soon, I think. She is a widow, and she also has a child.'

'If your family think that she is all right, I am sure everything will be fine. Many people get married like that. I read stories of people like that in the newspapers and magazines every day.'

'The woman is beautiful, they say, and the child an innocent little one.'

'Well, don't worry, Sayeed. You have many friends here, and most of them are married. We will all help you with any arrangements you wish to make.'

'At the moment I cannot think of anything. It all happened so suddenly, all at once, it is a shock.'

'The shock is yet to come,' Hameed laughed.

'Anyway, I am tired now, very tired. It has been a long journey. Can I sleep here tonight?'

'Yes, of course. I am sure Mohammad Rafi will not mind.'

'Where do you sleep?'

'I usually get a bed sheet, and put it on the floor in the room where they wash test tubes, and go to sleep there,' Hameed said.

'I could sleep in the chair.'

'Well, you are quite used to sleeping in these chairs,' Hameed said with another laugh. 'Here is a chair to put your feet on.' Hameed pushed a second armchair towards Sayeed. 'Shall I turn the lights off, Sayeed?'

'Do whatever you usually do.'

'I usually leave all these lights on. Can you sleep with them on?'

'Well, just turn off the ones in the sitting-room then.'

Hameed got up and turned off the lights in the sitting-room, and went next door to sleep.

Sayeed slid down the chair, pulled the second chair closer, put his feet on it, loosed his *gutra*, and covered his eyes with it.

Chapter 14

The city was quiet. Bright street lights illuminated the sky. Now and then an army or police vehicle would go slowly along the main airport road. Sometimes, the King's own secret police, in large black American limousines with darkened windows and long aerials on the roof, would whisper down the road. The city was asleep, even the man on the switchboard at the hospital, on a mat on the floor as usual.

Just before dawn, loud hailers tied to every mosque in the city started calling on the faithful to pray. It was about four in the morning as the men started coming out of their houses, walking half asleep towards their nearest mosque. The man at the hospital switchboard left it unattended and went to his prayer too.

Sayeed woke up when he heard the prayer call, and looked around the semi-dark sitting-room. Empty arm-chairs stood against the walls, there was a table in the middle of the floor, and two filing cabinets, one containing coffee and tea, and the other belonging to Abdul Mubarak. Hameed was not up yet. Sayeed was wondering whether to wake Hameed or go for his prayer wash. The prayer calls were still chanted. He felt guilty staying longer in his chair, and he was getting uneasy too. Sometimes the *mutawah* came in and caned anyone who did not go for prayers. But Sayeed still felt very tired. His whole body was aching. His legs, his back. And his right hand, which he had kept bent and tucked under his head on the metal arm rest, had become numb, and it hung lifelessly. He sat forward in his chair and kicked the other chair on which he had rested his feet. He rubbed his limp hand, clenched his fingers several times, and started to bend and stretch them. The prayer call had stopped when Sayeed got up and went to the sink for his wash.

As he was finishing, Hameed came in and made for the sink, scratching his head with both hands, dragging and thumping in his Japanese slippers.

'Sabah il-khayr, Hameed.'

'Sabah in-nuwr, Sayeed.'

'We're late.'

'Yes, let's go quickly.'

'I will be out soon. You go to the mosque. Did you sleep well?'

'Not bad. My back aches from sleeping in that chair,' Sayeed said, as he put his *gutra* on and started to walk towards the side door, which opened into the yard where the mosque was.

It was getting light outside. Sayeed left his slippers near the entrance to the mosque and walked on the sand with wet feet. When he got to the step, he stamped his feet on the concrete, and shook some of the sand off, and walked into the mosque, his sandy feet crackling on the plastic mat. Prayer had started. Sayeed stood next to the man from the hospital switchboard, and joined in. Soon Hameed came and stood next to him. Sayeed's thoughts were mixed. He needed help from everyone, so that he and his family could be happier, if it was the

Almighty's wish. He felt weak, as if his heartbeat had slowed down.

After the prayers, they all dispersed silently. Sayeed and Hameed walked towards the laboratory. The sun was not up yet, but the sky towards the east was getting lighter.

They went back to the sitting-room and Hameed switched on the kettle. He opened the filing cabinet and took out some peta bread and feta cheese.

'Would you like some bread?'

'I am hungry.'

'Eat this. There is some rice and lamb as well in the cabinet, left over from last night's supper.'

'I will have some bread and cheese,' Sayeed said.

'Sit here at the table, and put that newspaper on it.'

Sayeed sat at the table, and Hameed poured two glasses of very sweet tea, and put the bread and cheese on the newspaper.

'I am very tired still,' Sayeed said.

'You should go home.'

'I'm working today.'

'You could sleep in the chair here and no one will bother you.'

'I cannot sleep when people are around.'

'I don't think you have a problem there,' Hameed said.

They ate the dry bread with cheese, and sipped the hot tea.

'Soon everyone will be here,' Sayeed said.

'I don't think so. It is too early yet. They don't start till seven-thirty. But the patients will be here before that.'

'We can't do anything for them.'

'No, but they don't know that. They don't know one

worker from another. They think anyone who works here can take their blood, or give them their lab reports,' Hameed said.

'I know, I know. Stupid people. They can be very nasty and abusive. It makes you fed up.'

'Would you like to go back to the village?'

Sayeed laughed, but did not say anything. Hameed was surprised at how talkative Sayeed had become. Usually, he was a quiet person who hardly said much, and who conversed with nods, winks and grunts.

After breakfast Sayeed went back to the chair on which he had slept, pulled his legs under him and curled up.

'Ahh, sabah il-khayr, Sayeed,' someone said, walking into the sitting-room, and switching on the lights. Sayeed was woken up with a sudden shock. When he opened his eyes, and tried to discern what was happening, he saw Magidi looking down at him.

'Magidi! Kayf haalak?'

'Al-hamdulillah, shukran. When did you come back?'

'Last night. I slept here, because I came late.'

'You must be very tired.'

'Yes.'

'Good trip, was it?'

'Yes.'

'Your family all right?'

'Yes. They are fine.'

The patients were gathering outside.

'I had better have a glass of tea and a cigarette before they come in. Would you like some tea?' Magidi asked.

'No, I had a glass of tea a little while ago,' said Sayeed, sitting up in his chair and adjusting his *gutra*.

The laboratory staff started to come on duty. Some greeted Sayeed and asked him about the trip.

The routine work of the laboratory had started. Some of the staff who had had their tea went to their work places. Others still sat in the sitting-room, reading a book or newspaper. When Mohammad Rafi's voice was heard, everyone except Sayeed got up, and went to their work places. Abdul Mubarak came through the side door at the same time as Mohammad Rafi. He came into the sitting-room and put his pile of newspapers, which he got from the administration free of charge, on the table, gave a bear-hug to Sayeed, and kissed him on both his cheeks several times. He asked Sayeed how the trip had been, and Sayeed explained to him what had happened during the last few days back at the village. Abdul Mubarak gave a big laugh when he heard about the marriage plans, and Mohammad Rafi suppressed his laugh, but expressed his pleasure and wished him well before he went into his office.

'I am very glad for you,' Abdul Mubarak said.

'I am very worried!'

'Don't worry, there is nothing to it. I got married a few months ago, as you know, in a hurry, because the hospital administration was giving accommodation in the new block of flats only to married people. So I went and got married, and was given the marriage certificate all in one weekend but still they didn't give me a flat,' Abdul Mubarak said with some bitterness.

'They give most of the flats to foreign workers,' Sayeed said.

'Yes, I am still trying to get a flat there. They keep refusing to consider it.'

'Did you see the Director?'

'Many times. He is useless!'

'Well, there is no chance of a porter like me getting a hospital flat. I am hoping to make my hut bigger, with the help of some of my friends in the area where I live,' Sayeed said.

'I had better go and do some work,' Abdul said.

'Yes, otherwise Mohammad Rafi will shout at you.'

'Ahk. He cannot shout at me. He is a foreigner. This is our country, our hospital, yours and mine, Sayeed. He is working for us! He may be the chief, but if he shouts at me, I will shout at him louder,' Abdul Mubarak said, getting up from his chair.

'There was something I wanted to ask you,' Sayeed said.

'Tell me later.'

'This is something very important. I need your help,' Sayeed added, looking down and rubbing his hands together.

'What is it, Sayeed? Tell me now,' Abdul Mubarak said, sitting down next to him.

'I don't know how to say this, but there is no one else I can ask,' Sayeed said.

'Tell me anything you want, and I will do it, Sayeed. You are like my own brother. You are my brother. So, please tell me,' said Abdul Mubarak, patting Sayeed's back.

'I want to borrow some money. I do not have enough for all these wedding expenses.'

'Yes, you can borrow some money. That is not a problem at all. I will help you, we are all brothers, and I will help you. How much do you want to borrow?'

'About twenty thousand dinars.'

'What?' Abdul Mubarak said with surprise, leaning

backwards in his chair. 'That is a lot of money! I don't think I could lend you that much. I don't have that much. I thought you wanted a couple of thousand or so.'

'No, I need a lot of money. For the dowry, the wedding ceremony, jewellery, and other things I have to buy.'

'Don't you have any money?'

'I have about twenty thousand dinars, but that is not enough.'

'What about your brother?'

'He hasn't any.'

'Where do you keep your money?'

'It's with a friend of mine. He says he keeps it in a bank. He is a good boy, and he will let me have it whenever I want it.'

'I don't know what to do,' Abdul Mubarak said. 'But don't worry, I will think of something. Please don't worry. I must go to work now, otherwise we will get very far behind,' Abdul Mubarak said, getting up.

'All right, Abdul Mubarak. Please try. I will pay it off monthly.'

'Don't worry, Sayeed. Let me think of a way to raise this money,' Abdul Mubarak said, walking out of the sitting-room.

Later that morning, Abdul Mubarak discussed the matter with Mohammad Rafi while he was having his liver roll and a glass of tea, and they came to the conclusion that the only way to raise the money was to have a collection. So Abdul Mubarak went around explaining to everyone, as gently as possible, the desperate situation Sayeed was in, and asked them to contribute as much as they could, so that Sayeed could go ahead with his marriage. He was getting old, and he did not have much time left before he was too old, he told them.

Everyone promised to give something. One technician suggested that perhaps Abdul Mubarak might say to Sayeed that it was all from him, but the others said that they had to trust him, and even though Abdul was a nasty person, he could be trusted with that. Abdul Mubarak wrote down the names of the people who wished to contribute, and asked them to bring the money soon because Sayeed was going to the village in a week's time to arrange the shopping for the bride, and to make other wedding arrangements. It was a busy day for Abdul Mubarak.

It had been a very long day for Sayeed . Everyone had congratulated him. He had hardly done any work, except bring spiced liver rolls to several people in the laboratory.

Farial, the female Egyptian technician, and Dr Fatima could not believe Sayeed's wedding plan, and were whispering and giggling quietly, glancing at Sayeed, now and then, secretly. Abdul Mubarak burst into loud laughter while explaining about the collection to others who had not heard. Sayeed felt very disconcerted. He felt that everyone was talking about him. When it came to five o'clock, time to go, no one was happier than Sayeed.

Sayeed went upstairs to the administration offices, to put his thumbprint on the register, and went out to the main road to catch a bus home.

The roads were congested. The taxis and minibuses were full of passengers. The blaring noise of the radios and cassette players in the vehicles, the constant loud noise of the car horns, and the fast revving noise of the engines made the streets deafening. The sun's rays were still hot. Dust clouds made by the vehicles looked like mist, and this, combined with noxious exhaust fumes, was choking. Sweat was pouring from everyone, soaking their clothes. It evaporated fast, leaving salt crystals on the edges of the dust-covered sweat patches.

Sayeed stood by the main road. A Toyota truck stopped. The driver said where he was going. Sayeed was going further, but he accepted the lift, hoping to catch another ride for the rest of the journey. If he had walked on to the main bus station, he would have been able to get a lift directly to the place where he lived, and it would have been cheaper to have one direct ride, but he was tired. Sayeed agreed the fare, climbed on to the back of the truck, and leaned against a corner. There were a few other passengers on the truck. They all seemed tired after a day's work. Some of them looked as though they had worked outside on the roads. It did not take long for Sayeed to get another truck that went near his shanty area. By the time he had reached home, the sun was beginning to go down over the shanty huts on the horizon.

There were children playing on the track which ran from the main road to the hut area, and when they recognised Sayeed, one of the boys threw an empty can at him. It did not hit him. Sayeed kicked the can away, and walked on towards his hut.

He unbolted the door, kicking off the sand in front of the skirt of the door, so that he could open it, and entered the hut. A fine layer of sand covered everything inside. Sayeed took the mattress outside and shook it. He did the same to his pillows and his clothes. After the dusting, he locked the door and walked to the little shop in the shanty town for some water, bread, and a few other groceries. The sun had gone down, it was getting darker. The sky was reddish to the west, towards the city, and the huts were lit. On the way to the shop, Sayeed met a few of his neighbours. He told one of his friends about the wedding, and about the extension that he was thinking of for his hut. His friend told him that he must ask permission from the *mutawah* for the area, before any extensions or alterations could be made to any of the hovels in the shanty town. He said that he might have to pay him some money for his expenses. Sayeed was apprehensive about this, and asked his friend whether he could come with him to see the *mutawah*. His friend was willing to come. He even volunteered to help Sayeed with some building materials like sheets of tin and wooden boxes if he needed them. He could get these from the rubbish skips at his work place, and could bring them here in his own truck, he told Sayeed . They agreed to go and see the *mutawah* that evening.

When Sayeed and his friend went to see the *mutawah*, after the last prayer for the day, Sayeed saw the best dwelling in the whole area. Inside, it was well carpeted, and it was roomy. A desert cooler was fixed to one of the walls. After many cups of cardamom coffee, Sayeed managed to get permission to build an extension, and agreed to pay the *mutawah* one hundred dinars for his expenses. Sayeed was greatly relieved. He thanked the *mutawah*, and his friend, and went back to his hut. He went to sleep straight away, a happy man, but a tired one.

Chapter 15

Everyone in the laboratory and some in the administration offices, and others who knew Sayeed, got used to the idea that Sayeed would be married soon. Abdul Mubarak managed to collect about six thousand dinars in three days, and he was surprised at the amount some gave. Sayeed did not even know some of those who contributed, but they knew him and Abdul Mubarak well, so generous donations were collected. Still, it was far less than the twenty thousand dinars that Sayeed needed. Abdul Mubarak did not want to disappoint Sayeed, but it seemed impossible to collect that amount. After consulting Mohammad Rafi, Abdul Mubarak decided to speak to the hospital finance department to ask for a loan for Sayeed. At first the head of finance refused even to discuss the matter, because Sayeed's income was very low, but after persistent persuasion by Abdul Mubarak, he promised to consider a loan of ten thousand dinars, provided the director of the laboratory undertook to guarantee that the money would be paid back to the hospital within two years. Abdul Mubarak was pleased, and he went to discuss the matter with Mohammad Rafi, and with the director of the laboratory.

After Sayeed's thumbprints on a few documents, and

a guarantee from the director of the laboratory, and the final approval by the hospital director, Abdul Mubarak managed to get the loan for Sayeed, which he would have to pay back by monthly deductions from his salary.

Sayeed was glad, but he was worried about the monthly payments, and the reduction in income this would bring, especially when he needed more money to feed two more people.

The hut was another major worry for Sayeed, especially living in that crowded area, without a proper water supply. Back at the village, a water pump drew water from the wells and the water came out cool and fresh. Here it was a communal water tank. And dust and dirt blew through the gaps in the hut. All these things were worrying him. The hut was smaller than the smallest room in Latifa's house. He had tried to explain this to his family, but it was impossible to make them understand the hopelessness of finding some other accommodation, in a proper house or flat, because of the high rents which the landlords charged. There were always foreign workers who could afford to pay these rents, and there was a shortage of buildings to rent. The number of foreigners in the city was steadily growing. Sayeed was very apprehensive when he thought the bride and the child were coming to live in his hut. Ironically, he did not want the bride's family to know too much about this problem, just in case they would object to the marriage to which Sayeed was beginning to look forward. Everyone who came to the city gave up the comforts of the village, but they came thinking that the city was a place of luxury. Perhaps they might get used to the hut, he thought. The city was full of shops which had everything, imported from all over the world. The open markets were full of goods, beautiful clothes, toys for children, and those things should make them happy. They should compensate for the uncomfortable dwelling in the shanty town, he thought. But it was difficult for him to convince himself that everything would be all right. It will be God's will, he thought, and with that he felt a bit relieved, and decided to make the extension as big as possible.

His friend was very helpful. First they drew a plan on the sand: two bedrooms, one small one for the child and the other for his wife and him; a sitting-room at the front, and a kitchen at the back. The toilet would be a problem, because everyone went to the desert, and wiped themselves with sand. Sayeed wanted a small toilet built, just for his family, a few metres away from his hut, near the electricity pylon. The others in the shanty area would laugh, his friend had said, but Sayeed was determined to build a simple toilet. He wanted a hole a few metres deep dug in the sand, covered with planks, and a hole in the middle, and a shelter built around it. To avoid others using it, he wanted to fix a lock on the door.

Sayeed was hoping to go back to the village the following weekend, but he was busy building his extension. He managed to get three days off work, and with the help of his friend and a few neighbours, he built the extension and the toilet much more quickly than he had expected. Some building materials were collected from the desert and rubbish tips, the rest from his friend's work place. Planks of wood and roofing materials were bought at the market. They made the hut as draught-proof as possible, and they even managed to get a second-hand desert cooler fitted. He bought some cheap carpets, and covered the sandy floor, and got his hut connected to the communal electricity supply, and bought a refrigerator. He furnished the hut as best he could, and was a bit relieved. Now it seemed the hut was habitable. With a woman's touch, it would be a home, he thought.

He went back to the village with almost eighteen thousand dinars. Before he went, he asked his friend to take his money from the bank. He would need some of it for the dowry.

The two *thorbe*s that he had ordered were ready. Akila and Halima managed to sew two dresses each for themselves, and were busy sewing dresses for the children. Akila had gone with Latifa to buy white lace material for her wedding dress, and also helped her to sew her dresses. They were all excited. Latifa's parents were very sad, but the child did not know what was happening, and for her all this activity, and the visits from many people to the home, was enjoyable.

Latifa was very happy. Now and then she would sing quietly, but when she saw her parents, she went quiet. She was looking forward to the marriage. It had been some time since her husband had died. She was looking forward to the security of a married home and a husband.

She did not know how the child would react, or whether Sayeed would like her, and whether Sayeed's family would treat the child as one of their own. City life was something she was looking forward to. She had gone to the city with her late husband, and they had been to *souk*s there. It was thrilling to see the big shops with beautiful clothes, shoes from foreign lands, supermarkets full of goods, and people dressed in colourful dresses. She had seen big cars, gold shops with gold jewellery hanging from the ceiling and all around inside the shop and in glass cases. Millions of dinars' worth of gold, glistening and moving in a slight breeze, and the bustle of the crowd haggling, trying out bangles or necklaces. The beautiful solid gold hip decorations with wide gold belts, and flat gold attachments hanging all around them, and women sitting outside gold shops trying to sell some of their gold jewellery at a cheaper price. All this was exciting. She had heard that during wedding ceremonies in the city, some rich families hired belly dancers, and only the women and the bridegroom were allowed to watch. Village life was quiet, and it had become monotonous. Her only outing was when she went with her parents to the shops.

Sayeed spent some money on Latifa's jewellery, and gave the rest to Halima to look after. Mustafa sold some animals to get some money for his expenses. He also promised to provide some animals for the wedding feast which was going to be in Mustafa's house. Sayeed managed to persuade Mustafa to order a new *thorbe* for himself.

It was a busy weekend for Sayeed. With Mustafa he visited family friends in the village, and invited them to the wedding ceremony. Every time they visited friends' houses, they had to spend a long time drinking glasses of coffee, and talking. Some of their friends volunteered to prepare food, and wanted to give animals for the feast.

Halima was to look after all the arrangements, and Mustafa was to buy the rice and other necessary things, and he was to borrow big cooking pots, and serving dishes, carpets and mats from his friends in the village. They were expecting a large crowd, and some women in the village wanted to come and help Halima and Akila do the cooking.

Sayeed was satisfied with all the arrangements. He left for the city, and managed to get home before it was dark.

Chapter 16

The night was quiet. Latifa was woken up just after midnight. She had been sweating. When she remembered the nightmare she had had she started to shake uncontrollably. She dreamt that her little daughter Leila had been ill with a very high fever, and the child was hallucinating. She was asking for her father who had gone away to the city with a truckload of vegetables. Latifa's parents were sponging the little girl with cold water. Latifa was crying, quite helplessly. There was no doctor in the village. It was too far to the city, to the hospital. The child was too ill to travel. Then Latifa woke up and remembered that her husband was dead. She felt very frightened. The room was in semi-darkness, with only a very low night light in the corner on the floor. The wardrobe door was slightly ajar, and she could see her dead husband's clothes still hanging there. His long white *thorbe*s, and dark brown cape with gold threaded borders, and outside, to the left of the wardrobe, on the floor, his slippers, some new, and some old and worn out, as if he were still alive, and would be back soon. Latifa felt as if he was watching her and the child, who was sleeping next to her with her head on the small pillow, her little thumb just outside her half-open mouth, fast asleep, peaceful. Latifa's heart was beating faster, but the shaking stopped. She took her hand out of the blanket, and started to stroke the child's head. Leila's smooth soft hair was wet with sweat, and her face resembled her late father's. Slowly the child's face started to blur and Latifa's eyes filled with tears. They started flowing down her cheeks. She felt numb. The child pushed her thumb back in her mouth and started sucking. Latifa crawled closer to her, and put her face next to her, kissed her forehead, and started stroking her head. For her, it seemed the whole world had come to an end. Suddenly she felt very guilty. Her little girl did not understand what was going to happen. Latifa was to be married in two days' time, but still she felt the presence of her dead husband. It had not been very long.

Latifa tried to sleep, but could not. She could hear her mother next door, snoring loudly. It had been a warm night. She lifted the blanket, pushed it aside, and covering herself and the child instead with a thin sheet, she started fanning the child with the magazine that she had been reading before she had gone to sleep. She could hear the rustling noise of the leaves on the date palm trees outside, and a slight breeze came through the gaps in the window a few feet above their heads.

The decision to get married had been made, and there was no turning back now. Latifa thought it would be better if she could stay unmarried and bring up the child on her own. But they were poor. They needed money to buy food and clothes. Her mind was occupied with all these confused thoughts, and she felt that she had no choice in her future, which was God's will. The city was waiting for her. Perhaps a good school for her child, so that she could be educated. She read in the newspapers how the government was now trying to encourage girls to go to school and be educated, and Latifa's father believed that girls should be educated. He also believed that women should have a fair chance in life like men. He was very sorry that he had not been able to send Latifa to school. He himself had taught her to read and write. Her mother could do neither.

This second marriage would be a new step in her life. She was forced into it by circumstance. Now she was not sure that she wanted to go ahead with it. The memories of her late husband were still fresh, and a strong sense of betrayal shrouded her mind.

It was getting towards the early hours of the morning. The cockerels had started crowing. She heard a prayer call far away. She was too tired, and fell asleep slowly.

When she woke up, she found her mother sitting next to her.

'Ummi. what's the matter?' Latifa asked.

'Oh, I am all right. I just could not sleep.'

'How long have you been here?'

'Not very long,' her mother said with a sigh.

'You sound very sad, ummi.'

'Is there anything to be happy about? That old man is going to marry you, and he is going to take you away to the city. We will not be able to see you for a long time, that is if ever,' her mother said, and she started sobbing, covering her face with both hands.

'Don't worry, ummi, I will come and see you often, it takes only half a day to get here.'

'It's your father's fault. He agreed to give you away to that horrible old man. I tried not to say anything all this time, but I cannot keep it to myself any longer.'

'He is not that old. He looks old, but he is not old, Akila said, and she says that he is a very gentle man.

What we want is someone who will be kind to Leila. She misses her father still. She does not ask for him, but she has not completely forgotten him. She thinks that one day he will come back, with lots of sweets and toys.'

'Oh, this child! Our baby. How can your father and I live here without her, and without you? She is so attached to your father.'

'Don't worry, ummi, this is God's will. I think everything will be all right. Father is right. I cannot live without someone's support after you are both gone. Surely you don't want me to send Leila begging, do you?'

'Your father could have found someone younger, and a bit stronger. That man is like an earthworm.'

'Please, ummi, stop now. I am sure father knows what is best for all of us. He is a very clever person.'

'Yes, yes. You think he is clever, and his friends think he is clever too. He can read books. But let me tell you, he is not clever!' her mother shouted angrily.

'Please do not shout so loudly, he might hear.'

'He is asleep, like a log. Even if you beat drums, he will not wake up. He got up earlier, prayed and went back to sleep again.'

'Who else would want to marry a woman with a child, ummi?' Latifa asked sadly.

'Yes. They can marry four at a time. Ah, never mind. There must be justice in this somewhere,' her mother said.

'Our father only married you, ummi.'

'Yes, I suppose I shall have to be grateful to him for that. However, he is not a bad man. He is too kind, that is his problem. Let us pray before the child wakes up.'

Both women went to the middle of the room and

prayed. It was almost daylight, and the child was still fast asleep. Latifa got up and went to the kitchen with her mother who started to boil some water for coffee.

Latifa went through the kitchen door to the back of the house where the water tank was. She walked barefooted on the soft white sand, and looked at the garden which had date palms and fern trees all around it, and a vegetable garden in the middle. The water tank and the small hut that accommodated the water pump were next to the vegetable patch which was full of cucumbers, melons, pumpkins, and a large variety of other vegetables. The soil in the vegetable garden was still wet from the previous day's watering.

Latifa had grown up here, on this large piece of land. Both their neighbours' houses, on either side, were not far away, and they could see their houses through the trees, but could never hear any noise. When she was small, the neighbours' children used to come and play with her. Now they were all married and gone, some girls to the city, others to different parts of the village. She rarely came into contact with any of them now.

She tried to recall the games that they had played in the garden. Her father used to get annoyed when they trampled any of his plants. They would climb the trees in the garden which were not so tall then. Those were happy days, Latifa thought. Then she remembered how her husband had helped her father to cultivate the land. He had bought the water pump. Before that they used to pull the water by hand from the deep well. It was exhausting. Her husband used to take the vegetables from the farm, and from other farms in the village, to the nearby towns and to the city in his truck. They were newly married then, and full of hope for the future. He was kind to her and her parents, and they liked him too. No one would replace him, she thought.

She went towards the hedgerow, and plucked a red Chinese rose from one of the bushes. She smelled the flower. It reminded her of her youth. One of her friends had shown her how to pull the gynoecium out of the flower and taste the honey at the base of it. She could still remember the sticky clear liquid with the mild, sweet taste, and its fragrance. They used to wear these flowers in their hair and pretend that they were little princesses.

Latifa walked towards the water tank, holding the stalk of the flower between her forefinger and thumb, twisting it, and smelling it, now and then. The morning was cool and fresh, and it was quiet everywhere.

She put the flower on the concrete wall of the water tank, and took a metal bucket, filled it with water, and threw the bucketful of water at the flower. The flower fell down, and its crushed petals were covered with wet sand. Then she put her bare right foot near the flower, and with her toes threw the flower as far as she could, and came back to the water tank, filled the bucket with water again, and washed her face.

Chapter 17

Sayeed had brought a few boxes of cakes from the city. He had also brought presents for the children. Halima had taken over the organising of the wedding, and Akila was helping her. They managed to get all the dresses ready for the children, and sent Mustafa to do the shopping, and to borrow things from their friends in the village. Mustafa's lifestyle had changed slightly. He had not been able to get his afternoon sleep for a few days, and he was feeling very tired and irritable. The women were organising the wedding ceremony the way they wished, and Mustafa's opinions were ignored by both wives who now seemed united and friendly. When Sayeed came home, Mustafa was relieved, because he could now let Sayeed do some of the work, and he could relax.

Family friends dropped in to see how they could help, but whenever they came, they stayed for a long time. Coffee had to be served, and long hours were spent in talking to them. Most of them were more of a hindrance than a help, the women thought. Some of the women who had come were quite useful, they helped Halima and Akila to clean and tidy up the house.

The day before the wedding Mustafa killed four goats and a few chickens. The boys and Sayeed helped him to get the meat ready. The skins of the goats' heads were carefully removed, leaving the eyes still in the sockets. Several containers were filled with freshly cut and washed meat, and were taken to the kitchen. Halima and Akila and some of the women from the neighbourhood started cooking. They had decided to delay the boiling of the rice until a few hours before the wedding ceremony, so that they could serve it fresh.

The wedding ceremony was held at night. The bridegroom's party went to collect the beautifully dressed bride in white, and Mustafa handed over the dowry to Latifa's father. Latifa and her parents were crying, and the child started crying loudly too. Several suitcases were packed and ready, and they were loaded on to the convoy of trucks, and the bride and bridegroom were seated in one of the guests' cars. Latifa's parents and the child were in another car. They all came to Mustafa's house, and when the bride and the bridegroom were getting out of the car, all the women started making loud hooting noises and tapping their mouths with their hands.

The feast was held in a grand way in the brightly lit garden beside the date palm grove. Carpets were laid on the ground, and men and women sat on separate sides. There was plenty to eat and plenty of soft drinks and cardamom coffee. The party went on till the early hours of the morning, when the guests and the hosts could not eat any more. Some men danced, swinging their scimitars in the air and pretending to fight. The women sat with their faces covered, laughing and giggling, the bride among them. Sayeed sat next to Mustafa and the other men.

Leila sat curled up on Latifa's father's lap with tired

eyes. She had slept earlier on in the evening, but the noise had woken her up. She was watching the men dance on the carpets laid on the sandy yard.

Latifa was escorted into Sayeed's old room by Akila and some of her friends. They had decorated the room, and a new mattress and pillows were arranged in a corner. Earlier, Latifa's friends had organised her wardrobe, and the dresses that she had brought were hanging there. A few of Sayeed's clothes hung in a corner of the same wardrobe. The women left Latifa in the room, shut the door and went out.

Sayeed was reluctant to leave his friends. Mustafa suggested dragging him along and pushing him into the room. All the others agreed to this, and they burst out laughing. Sayeed got up quickly and with a wide smile on his face, went inside the house, and into the room. Mustafa came behind him slowly and locked the door. Sayeed started banging on the door, but Mustafa went away laughing. They started beating the drums again, and some started to sing, and all the men started dancing.

Sayeed turned towards the bride, who was sitting on the floor. The main light in the room was on, and Sayeed saw Latifa's face for the first time.

The following morning Akila and Halima woke up early, and got the breakfast ready. Latifa and Sayeed slept late. When everyone was up they all sat in the sitting-room and had breakfast.

Sayeed wanted to leave for the city as soon as possible, but Mustafa was asking him to stay with them for one more day and go the following day. But Sayeed wanted to go that day, and everyone had to agree to that. They had all had very little sleep the night before, and were tired.

Latifa's parents, who had gone back home during the early hours of the morning, came back soon after Mustafa's family had finished their breakfast, and they brought Leila with them. Some of her toys and dresses were packed in cardboard boxes tied with string. Leila was glad to see her mother, and clung on to her when she saw her. Latifa started weeping, and she looked at the sad face of the child whom she had not seen for a few hours. They told the child that her mother would be going on a long journey in a truck, and she would be going with her. The child's face lit up. Then she asked her mother whether her grandparents were coming as well, and Latifa said they were coming later. The child looked sad and raised her hands towards her grand-father who took her from Latifa's hand, hugged and kissed her on both cheeks, and squeezed her gently. The child clung on to him, tucked her head under the chin of the old man, put her thumb in her mouth, and started stroking his newly hennaed beard.

They all helped to load the truck that was parked near the verandah. The older boys helped Mustafa and Sayeed to load the large suitcases and boxes, and the women carried the smaller bags and boxes. The little children were fighting with each other to help carry things, but most of the items were too heavy for them.

Latifa kissed her parents, and hung on to her mother, and they both started sobbing. Halima and Akila were standing next to Leila, and they in turn hugged and kissed her. Latifa said she would be back soon to see them, and got into the truck with her child.

Mustafa got in and started the engine. Sayeed shook hands with Latifa's father, who hugged Sayeed and kissed him on both cheeks. 'Please . . . my daughter . . . look after her. Please,' Latifa's father begged.

Sayeed told him not to worry, that he would look after her. He waved to everyone, got into the pick-up, and shut the door. The truck started to move, they all turned back and waved to those who were standing at the front of the house.

Mustafa slowly drove the truck on to the dust track. Latifa was wiping her tears, and the child was screaming and trying to look outside over Sayeed's shoulders, through the window, through the dust cloud, to see whether she could still see her grandparents.

Sayeed was quiet. He put his hand in his pocket, and took a handful of sweets, and showed them to the child. She looked at them, turned her head the other way and continued sobbing. Sayeed clenched his hand and put the sweets back into his pocket. Mustafa was tired, and was driving slowly. The traffic was heavy on the main road.

They stopped several times, for petrol, for food and toilets. Latifa was quiet, and was very shy and embarrassed. She was with two males whom she hardly knew. Her husband whom she had seen only once before her wedding was still a stranger. She was careful not to say much because she did not know what would be offensive to them. She kept her face covered with her black veil. She did not know how religious her husband or her brother-in-law were. They were quiet, and cautious, and did not want to make Latifa unhappy. Mustafa knew about women. Sayeed had still to learn. At one of the stops, Leila asked her mother to buy her a doll. Sayeed quickly got it for her. He also bought her sweets. The child tasted the sweets and smiled at Sayeed. He nodded his head, and the child hid behind her mother. Latifa looked at Sayeed and smiled. He was happy, because the child was not unhappy any more.

It was dusk when they came to the area of the city where Sayeed lived. The street lights were on, and the vehicles on the road had their head lamps on. Sayeed had to direct Mustafa, because it was the first time he had been to the place where Sayeed lived. They turned to the road which led to the shanty town. The street lights stopped at the main road, and the tarred road continued towards the army camp, towards the National Guard primary care hospital unit beyond it. Then the tarred road stopped, and a dust track continued towards the shanty town. They saw the lights that came from the huts in the shanty town which spread several square miles to the right, towards the city. To the left was the empty desert where the Bedouins camped.

Mustafa saw the small huts that were scattered everywhere, and could not believe that Sayeed lived in one of them, nor that he could bring his bride and the child to live there. He did not say anything, he did not turn his head to look at Latifa's face through the veil either.

'This is the right area, Sayeed, is it?' Mustafa asked.

'Turn to the right there, just near that electricity pylon. That place with a new roof is my home,' Sayeed said.

'That place? But I thought . . .' Mustafa said.

'I told you how difficult it is to get a house in the city. This is temporary. We will look for a house soon,' Sayeed reassured him.

Latifa was quiet. Mustafa stopped the truck in front of the hut, and Sayeed opened the door, went inside and switched on the lights and the desert cooler.

'I am sorry it is small, but it's temporary. This is the city,' Sayeed said to Latifa. She did not say anything, but walked in and looked at the sitting-room, then the bedrooms and the kitchen. Mustafa looked at Sayeed and shrugged his shoulders.

Latifa opened the back door, and looked at the back garden which was sandy, and littered with rubbish. At the end of the back garden, to the right, towards the electricity pylon, was the toilet which Sayeed had built. To the left, the next-door neighbour's goat herd was caged in, and the children were feeding them.

Latifa wiped her eyes, went into one of the bedrooms with her child, and sat on the floor. Mustafa took Sayeed near the truck. 'I don't understand you, Sayeed. This is not even big enough for animals,' Mustafa said.

'I know that. Don't you think I did not try? It is very expensive to get a flat or a house here. All this happened in such a hurry, and the rents are very high,' Sayeed said.

'People in the village think that you have brought her to a decent place. I don't know what to say to them when I go back,' Mustafa said.

'Say what you like. Best thing is not to say anything. Answer the questions that they ask. Then it is simple. Say this is temporary. I don't want to live here either. On the other hand, look at all those thousands of people who live in these huts. Most of them are from villages, and some of them have bigger houses there than ours. I have some friends here. This is the city. It is different. It is hard. It is certainly not like village life. People have to get used to it. I got used to it, and given time they will get used to it as well,' Sayeed said.

'I doubt that they will ever get used to it, Sayeed. Let

us unload the luggage. I certainly don't know where you are going to put all these things. They will take up a lot of room. I could take some of these back, if you want me to,' Mustafa offered.

'No, no, we will find space somewhere. Let us unload it, get some food, and some sleep,' Sayeed said.

'I cannot eat anything. After unloading I will sleep in the truck, and go back tomorrow morning. Ask Latifa whether she would like to eat,' Mustafa said.

Latifa said that she was not hungry. The child was asleep on her lap. Mustafa and Sayeed unloaded the luggage, and piled everything in the sitting room. Sayeed showed Latifa the outside toilet, and the few plastic containers of water that he had in the kitchen. Latifa did not say much, but prepared a mattress for herself and the child, and covered it with one of the blankets that they had brought with them, and went to sleep.

Mustafa sat in the truck, smoked a few cigarettes and went to sleep on the seats.

Some of the neighbours came to see what was happening, and Sayeed explained that he had brought his family. Some of the women wanted to come and see Latifa, but Sayeed said that she was sleeping.

Sayeed went inside, into the smaller bedroom, and went to sleep on the mat on his own.

Chapter 18

Latifa felt the cold draught that came through the wall. It was noisy. The hut started shaking slightly as the wind blew through the electricity pylon. Leila was fast asleep. Latifa covered the child's face with her black veil which she had left near the mattress. Small gushes of dust were coming into the hut. In the other room, Sayeed started to cough, and Latifa covered her nostrils and mouth with the blanket.

It was dark outside. The goats in the neighbour's pen were noisy. Latifa got up, took the toilet key which was hanging on a nail on the kitchen wall, opened the back door, and went out. She could see the silhouetted shapes of the huts in the neighbourhood, and the electricity pylon. She came back and filled one of the plastic buckets with water from a large can, and walked barefooted towards the toilet. The cables of the electricity pylon were swinging gently. The wind was dying down. Towards the city the sky was bright, but there was no sign of the sun yet. She walked on the soft sand, and opened the door of the toilet and went in. The coarse wooden floor with a hole in the middle was damp. She felt a shiver down her spine, and her feet were itchy. The smell in the toilet was unbearable. When she entered, some flies came out of the toilet hole, buzzing. Cockroaches on the floor dispersed quickly. Latifa felt sick. She was shaking off the flies. She felt as if all her sensations were focused on her feet. She stood on her toes, on the damp, wooden, slimy floor. When she came out of the toilet, she started wiping her feet violently on the sand, rubbing it all over her feet to clean around them. She walked towards the hut as fast as she could, got some water out of the water can, and washed her feet. Then she found some soap, and she lathered them well, then rinsed them again. Even the thought of that toilet was making her sick. She opened her handbag which was on a cushion in the bedroom, took out a bottle of perfume, and held it to her nostrils.

Latifa was angry. She was angry with her parents, with Akila, and with her dead husband too. She felt that they were all responsible for the suffering which she thought had already begun.

She sat on the mattress and started to cry. The wind had died down. Sayeed was quiet in the other room. The child was fast asleep. She covered her with the blanket, and took the veil off her face. It was quiet everywhere. Latifa put her head on the pillow again, and went to sleep.

She was woken up by the morning prayer call. Sayeed got up and went to the kitchen. Mustafa came around the hut towards the back entrance, and Sayeed brought some water outside. While one was pouring water the other washed himself for the prayer, and when both had finished they walked towards the mosque. Latifa got up, had her wash and prayed in her room. It was getting lighter now. After the prayer Latifa lit the gas cooker and started to boil some water for coffee.

Sayeed introduced Mustafa to the *mutawah* while they were coming out of the mosque. The *mutawah* had a long white beard, and wore a brown cape with gold-threaded borders. He was carrying a long cane which reached his shoulders. He was pleased to hear that Sayeed had settled down, and he said that he would send his wife to meet Latifa to ask whether she would need any help with anything. Sayeed was too humble to refuse this offer. Both brothers walked to the little shop in the shanty town, and bought some peta bread, feta cheese and pickles. Mustafa bought a packet of Rothmans, and they both walked back to the hut. Everyone was looking at Mustafa. Sayeed's friends greeted them and invited them to their dwellings.

Latifa had made a jug of coffee, and Sayeed and Mustafa sat in the sitting-room and ate their breakfast. Latifa took some bread to her bedroom, and ate a few pieces with cheese. The child was still asleep.

As soon as Latifa had finished her breakfast, she started dusting and tidying up the room. She asked Sayeed to find some old newspapers to plug the gaps in the wall to stop dust blowing in. Sayeed said that he did not buy any newspapers, but promised to bring some from the hospital. The neighbours fed the goats with their newspapers.

The child woke up. She seemed excited about the new place. She wanted to go outside and play in the sand. Latifa insisted that she should eat something and have a glass of milk before she went out. The child ate a few small pieces of bread soaked in milk and sugar, and went outside to play.

Latifa rearranged everything, unpacked some of the boxes, filled some of the cupboards, and hung their clothes in the plastic zip-up wardrobe in the corner of the bedroom.

'I ought to make a move,' Mustafa said.

'What's the hurry? You could go after lunch,' Sayeed suggested.

'No, no. If I leave now, I might be able to get home before dark. I am sure I will get lost in the city,' Mustafa said.

'It's easy, but stop and ask someone if you get lost,' Sayeed said.

'Sister, I am going,' Mustafa said.

'Brother, please do not tell anyone back home about this place. They might get worried,' Latifa said.

'We are going to look for another soon,' Sayeed promised.

'Don't worry too much. I will bring my women and children to visit you all soon. Then perhaps we can go to the desert for a picnic,' Mustafa said.

'If you can, bring my parents as well. Not so soon, perhaps after we have found a better place,' Latifa said.

'Make some friends around here. Then you will not feel so lonely,' Mustafa said.

'The whole area is smelly. The children look as if they have never had a wash in their lives. The women look old and their clothes are very dirty,' Latifa said.

'Most of these are poor people. Some keep goats or sheep. Their husbands go to the city to work as labourers on building sites, and they have very little money, but they are good people,' Sayeed said.

'I had better go now,' Mustafa said, lighting up a cigarette, and throwing away the burning match on to the sand. He got into his truck, adjusted his *gutra*, and reversed towards the open area away from the huts, turned around, and drove away towards the city.

Sayeed and Latifa walked back inside. It was cooler there. The air was still, and Leila was playing with her doll in the sand just outside the sitting-room window.

Latifa sat cross-legged near the desert cooler, and Sayeed sat near the window and watched the child playing.

'Where is everyone?' Latifa asked.

'It's getting hot. I think most people are still inside. Probably some of the women have gone to the desert with their animals, and some of the men have gone to the city,' Sayeed said.

'The smell around here is very bad. Why is that?' Latifa asked.

'They throw all their rubbish just outside their huts, and also the children go to the toilet near their huts, and cover it with sand.'

'I feel sick.'

'You will get used to the smell. After a few days, you won't notice anything,' Sayeed said with a laugh.

'I have a headache, I have been feeling sick all morning. Never in my life again will I go out without any slippers on my feet,' Latifa said.

Sayeed laughed.

'Back home I always walk around in the house, and in the garden barefooted,' Latifa said.

'I did the same back at the village. But it is different down here,' Sayeed said. 'Would you like to go to the city this evening?'

'Yes, very much. But how do we get there? You said women are not allowed on any public transport.'

'I will ask a neighbour of mine, Hussain Hasmi. He

usually goes to the city every evening. He is a young boy, a bit mischievous. He drives his truck very fast.'

'Well, young boys are like that. How old is he?'

'Oh, maybe about twenty. I don't know. He decorated his truck, inside and out. It is carpeted all over inside, the steering wheel, dashboard, the floor, the sides, and everywhere with red carpets.'

Latifa laughed. 'I have seen cars like that, back at the village. Those youngsters are crazy. What does he do?' Latifa asked.

'He works at the motor vehicle licence office in the city. Really, he should get married soon. But he says he has no money. He spends a lot of money on cars. That's why he does not have much. He has a lot of friends, they all dress up well, and go to the city almost every evening,' Sayeed said.

'Will he have room in his truck for us?' Latifa asked.

'Most probably. If any of his friends are going they can sit at the back of the truck. He is a good boy. I have known him since I first came to live here. He helped me to build this extension,' Sayeed said.

'Can I cook something?' Latifa asked.

'Please do. I don't know what there is to cook. It is almost midday, the shop must be closed now,' Sayeed said.

'I could cook some rice if there is any. Leila likes rice,' Latifa said.

'There should be some in the cupboard. I bought some before I went to the village. Have a look anyway,' Sayeed said.

Latifa found some rice. In the freezer section of the refrigerator she found some lamb. She cooked both, and the cooking smell camouflaged the unpleasant smells in the air. After the meal, Sayeed went to his little bedroom and went to sleep on his mattress. Latifa unpacked a few more boxes.

Chapter 19

The windows in Sayeed's hut were shut. Latifa was combing Leila's hair, brushing out the sand. The desert cooler was noisy, and was blowing damp, cold air. Earlier in the afternoon, the generator that supplied electricity for the ten huts in the corner of the shanty town where Sayeed lived had stopped. The old man who was looking after it had forgotten to refuel it. The neighbours found the old man sleeping. He refuelled the tank, and restarted the generator.

Hot dry air was coming through the gaps and cracks in the hut walls.

Soon after the afternoon prayer, Latifa made some tea, and they both sat in the sitting-room cross-legged, facing each other, drinking hot sweet tea in small clear glasses with little handles. They sat silently, occasionally lifting the glasses to sip the tea. Sayeed did not know what to say, and Latifa did not know how to start a conversation. He seemed to be in deep thought. He kept looking at the child who sat on Latifa's lap, quietly sucking her thumb.

Sayeed cleared his throat, and took a deep breath.

'It is very hot today,' he said.

'The heat is different here in the middle of the desert. It's a dry heat. Back home, you sweat a lot, and it is very uncomfortable, but here your skin does not retain the sweat, and it is bearable,' Latifa said.

'Hmm. I am sorry, Latifa. I know that this is quite a shock for you, but I promise I will start looking for another place soon,' Sayeed said.

'It's the smell, the dirt and the dust. This is almost like camping in the desert. I will go mad if I stay here too long. So, please take me out of here soon, or I will go back to my parents and wait there until you find a place,' Latifa said with tears in her eyes.

'You came here only yesterday, please be patient. All this was arranged in a hurry, and I need a lot of money for everything. Let us not talk about it any more,' Sayeed said, putting down his glass of tea on the metal tray in front of him.

They heard some voices just outside their hut, and Sayeed heard the *mutawah* calling for him. Sayeed got up quickly, and Latifa pulled her veil over her face, and went into her bedroom. He opened the front door. The *mutawah* was with his wife and their elder daughter who was married to a taxi driver who worked in the city.

'Please come in, mutawah,' Sayeed said.

Sayeed guided the women to the bedroom where Latifa was. The child followed them.

Sayeed and the *mutawah* sat cross-legged on the floor facing each other, and the *mutawah* took out his prayer beads and started twiddling with them, swinging his body slowly, forwards and backwards, smiling at Sayeed.

'Your house is quite big,' the *mutawah* said.

'It's rather small for all three of us. Anyhow, thank you for giving me permission to build the extension,' Sayeed said.

'Everyone wants to make his house bigger. Unless we go further into the desert, there is not much space,' the *mutawah* said.

'That's the problem with city life. Too many foreigners. They take all the available houses. Our people build them fast, but always give them to foreigners and charge very high rents,' Sayeed said.

'Foreigners are bad. They are a bad influence on our people. The radios, televisions, all these things are bad. People do not read religious books any more. They read newspapers and other books that corrupt the mind,' the *mutawah* warned.

'Of course, not all people get corrupted,' Sayeed said.

'No! But some of the young people growing up now do not have any respect for their elders any more, and I see a few of them in our area too. All they want is to dress up well, and drive a big car or something. Foreign women go out without covering their hair or faces. Soon our women will want to do the same,' the *mutawah* said.

'Yes, but you would not allow it, would you?' Sayeed said with a smile.

'Thank God we have the religious police. We can cane them. I heard one *mutawah* in the city centre cut a white woman's hair because she went to a supermarket without covering her hair.'

Sayeed laughed, and the *mutawah* looked animated.

'We must not let them corrupt our people,' the *mutawah* said, hitting the carpet with his cane. 'I will cane any woman in this area I see going out without covering her face and hair,' he said loudly.

Latifa brought a tray with two glasses of tea, and

placed it between the men. The *mutawah* thanked her. She shook her head slowly and withdrew quietly into the bedroom.

'Good tea. Plenty of sugar,' the *mutawah* said, taking a sip and smacking his lips.

'It's a very big change for my wife and the little child. I hope they get used to it and settle down soon,' Sayeed said.

'It will take time. We all come here from villages and we dislike it to start with, then after some time we get used to it. That's life. The government is going to build houses for us we hear. How long that will take I don't know. But when they build them, we will all be comfortable.'

'Yes, when they build them! Have you seen the half-built housing complex near the headquarters of the National Guard? They say it was stopped because the construction company went bankrupt,' Sayeed said.

'No, the real reason is it was too near the military headquarters. They don't want too many people near there.'

'I am going to take them to the city this evening,' Sayeed said.

'How are you going to get there? I could ask my son-in-law to take you, when he comes home later on.'

'I am hoping to ask Hussain Hasmi to take us.'

'Hussain Hasmi! Are you sure? I do not like that boy very much. He is a corrupt young man. His mind is not very good; he is not very religious at all. Sometimes I have to chase him into the mosque to pray,' the *mutawah* said.

'He's not a bad boy. He is very helpful to me. Youngsters are like that these days. Too many changes happen

to them and to their friends. Most of them are like that,'
Sayeed said.

'He must not forget what we are. All this is because of
foreign influence. He works with foreigners.'

'There are foreigners in the hospital where I work, but
they do not influence us. Some of them are quite good
people,' Sayeed said.

The *mutawah* did not say anything. He took a sip of
tea, put the glass down, and started toying with his
prayer beads.

'Now you have a wife, you should not have too
much to do with him. I keep telling him to get
married, but he says that he does not have the money,'
he said.

'He is like my brother. He may behave differently, but
he is very good at heart,' Sayeed said.

'Anyhow, do not forget what I said. I am older than
you and I have read a lot of religious books. He has taken
the path to the devil!' the *mutawah* said, pointing his
finger at Sayeed.

'Would you like some more tea, mutawah?'

'No, I am all right. I think we had better go now.
Please call my family.'

Sayeed slowly got up.

'Thank you very much for coming. It's a privilege to
have you in my house,' he said, wringing his hands.

He knocked on the bedroom door and told Latifa that
the *mutawah* was leaving.

The two female visitors came out of the bedroom, and
started following the *mutawah*, who was walking towards
the front door. 'You must come and visit us soon,' the
mutawah said.

'Thank you very much,' Sayeed said.

'Please come tomorrow night,' the *mutawah*'s wife said to Latifa.

'I am going to work tomorrow, and I do not know what time I will be back. Perhaps in two or three days' time I shall be free,' Sayeed said.

'All right. Do not worry, we will look after your family while you are at work,' the *mutawah*'s daughter said, holding Latifa's hand. 'You could come and see us while Sayeed is at work,' she said to Latifa.

Latifa kissed both the female visitors and they left.

'Very nice people. I feel very happy now,' Latifa said.

'They are all nice people here. I am sure they will be kind to you,' Sayeed said with a smile. 'Do you still want to go to the city today?'

'Yes, Sayeed. It will be a change. I do not want to buy anything, but I would like to look around the souks,' Latifa said.

'All right. I don't know whether I will be able to arrange any transport, but I will ask Hussain Hasmi when he comes home after work,' Sayeed said.

'Please,' Latifa said.

The child was hungry. Latifa took some leftover rice and meat and started feeding her.

Chapter 20

It was dusk. The lamps in the huts were lit. In the distance, on the main road, the street lights were lit. All the cars had their head lamps on, and the sky was getting darker.

Latifa was ready. She had put on one of her new dresses and new shoes. The child was ready too.

Sayeed had gone to see Hussain Hasmi. If he could not find Hussain, Sayeed was thinking of walking towards the main road with his wife and the child, about two kilometres away, and stopping a taxi to take them to the city. Hussain had just come home when Sayeed arrived, and he was very happy to help. He usually came home after work, got changed, and went to the city. As it happened, he wanted to go to the cloth *souk* as well, to buy some presents for a female cousin of his who lived in another village, and who was going to get married to one of his friends from his work place. Hussain was the matchmaker. Perhaps Latifa could help him select several pieces of material which his cousin could use to make her dresses, he said to Sayeed. Sayeed was glad he could return the favour.

Hussain Hasmi came in his new cream Toyota truck, stopped it near Sayeed's hut, flashed his lights, and blew the horn several times. Sayeed came out, raised his hand to Hussain, went in again and called Latifa. The child came running out, and Latifa followed her. She wore a black *abaya* which covered her body from head to toe. Sayeed locked the front door and came to the truck.

'Salaam alaykum, Hussain,' Sayeed said.

'Wa-alaykum is-salaam, Sayeed. Please get in,' Hussain said.

Sayeed got in first, and sat next to Hussain. Then the child got in, followed by Latifa who shut the door after her. Hussain blew the horn again, and started the truck. He went fast, creating a cloud of dust behind him, one hand on the steering wheel, the other on the cassette player. An Egyptian woman was singing a lament, backed by a full orchestra playing Western and Middle Eastern instruments.

Hussain drove fast, and when he came to the tarred road the truck lifted off into the air slightly, then landed back on the road.

'Salaam alaykum, sister,' Hussain said, leaning forward and looking over at Latifa.

'Wa-alaykum is-salaam, brother.'

'How are you?'

'Fine.'

'How do you like the city?'

'I haven't seen much of it yet.'

'You will like it. I am sure you will like it. It's not like the village. The city is lively. Everything happens here. So many things to look at. You can buy anything you want.'

'I hear everything is very expensive.'

'That may be true. I was only ten years old when my family came to the city, so I don't know much about village life. I like it here. All my friends are here,' Hussain said.

Hussain's air-conditioner was blowing cold air. Latifa's new perfume smelled fresh.

Sayeed was silent. Latifa showed the child a large amusement park on the side of the road as they passed. There were two of everything. Big Wheel, merry-go-round, all in duplicate. On one side was the entrance for men and boys, on the other side was the one for women and girls. The whole area was lit up with brightly coloured lights.

'I have been there,' Hussain said, laughing. 'They have a big earthworm. When you go on that your stomach turns upside down, it turns and twists so fast,' Hussain said.

'I would like to take Leila there one day. I haven't seen anything like that before,' Latifa said.

'I heard it is very expensive to go there,' Sayeed said.

'That's true. You pay something to go in, then if you want a ride on anything, you pay separately,' Hussain said.

The road was getting busier as they neared the city. It was completely dark now, but the street lights and the lights from the traffic and from the buildings lit up the whole city and the sky above it.

The traffic was heavy towards the *souk* area, and it took a long time for Hussain to find a parking place. Cars were parked on every possible space, on the roads and on the pavements. There were police directing the traffic. They were not allowing anyone to park near the big mosque on the square where they punished criminals, sometimes by beheading, after the midday prayers on Fridays. The clock tower stood at the opposite end of the square, and in between was the car park. The *souk* area was next to the clock tower. A wide street full of shops that sold only watches ran from near the clock tower towards the old mud fort, which was now a museum, protected and guarded by the National Guard.

In the cloth *souk,* shops with air-conditioners and desert coolers displayed bright-coloured materials imported from all over the world. Bales of cloth were rolled, or piled up in the shops, and the women customers made the salesmen open the bales. Then they would hold the material against their bodies, smell it, feel it with their hands and faces, ask each other's opinion, then leave it and go to other shops, and do the same thing all over again. Some women did buy material, in small quantities, or a bale at a time if they thought it was a bargain, after a great deal of haggling. They would then walk back to their vehicles behind their husbands, the bales of cloth balanced on their heads.

Sayeed and Hussain walked first, Latifa and Leila following. They walked past the clock tower, and the traffic policeman. They passed the washing-machine shops which were next to the radio and television shops, and walked towards the watch street. From there they turned left into a small lane which led into the cloth *souk.*

Latifa walked with the child, looking into the shops on both sides of the narrow lanes, seeing the variety and amount, amazed by it and envious of the rich women who walked in groups, their female servants walking mutely behind, carrying heavy loads, but unable, like Latifa, to afford the expensive goods themselves.

The shops were very busy. Latifa looked at several small dresses for Leila, and chose two short ones with short sleeves, and a pair of small plastic shoes which were shaped like little rabbits and made squeaky noises every time the child took a step. She looked at some material for herself, felt its soft smoothness on her face, on her lips, and on her fingertips, and wished that she had enough money to buy any cloth she liked, perhaps the whole shop, she thought.

The last prayer call started broadcasting from the big loud hailers on the mosque. The *mutawah*s and the religious police, all carrying long canes, came out into the shopping areas, and started driving the males into the mosque for the prayers. All the shopkeepers started to pull their shutters down quickly to avoid the *mutawah*s coming into their shops and hitting them with their canes. Some traders closed their shops, went into the back and drank tea, others obeyed the prayer call, went and had their prayer wash, and went to the mosque. Foreigners who belonged to other religions stayed behind. But sometimes the *mutawah*s would try to chase them to the mosque too, not knowing whether they were Muslims, and some of them ended up in the mosque, for fear of the *mutawah*s, and imitated prayer like the others in case the *mutawah*s humiliated them by caning them in public.

Sayeed and Hussain went to pray. Latifa sat on a step just outside one of the clothes shops. Hot air from the air-conditioners' exhaust pipes was blowing into the lanes. This, combined with the heat in the atmosphere and the poor ventilation in the lanes, stifled everyone. Some poor children who had run away when the *mutawah*s came, leaving their basins with Pepsi and 7Up cans wedged in between blocks of ice, had come back while the *mutawah*s were praying, and were making a small trade selling them to the women who were left behind.

Latifa and Leila shared a can of Pepsi. The lanes were almost empty. All the shops were shut.

After the prayers, all the men and small boys came back. The traders opened the shops, the lanes became crowded, and the whole place grew lively again.

Latifa bought a long dress for herself, and helped Hussain select a few materials for his cousin.

'How do you like the souk?' Hussain asked Latifa.

'So many shops, so many beautiful things, but they are all very expensive,' Latifa said.

Then they heard raised voices coming from one of the shops nearby. People started gathering. The shopkeeper was accusing a man of trying to steal. Other shoppers and shopkeepers joined the accuser. They started pushing the man, and shouting insults and abuse at him. The man was begging them to let him go. Then he started to cry.

'A mistake,' he said. He was not stealing, he only touched it. 'Please let me go,' he pleaded. But the crowd was becoming animated, like a lynch mob. Hussain went over before Sayeed could stop him.

'Please let that man go,' Hussain said, but his voice was drowned in a storm of abuse.

'Please, he has not taken anything. If he goes to court, and gets convicted, they will order his hand to be cut off. Please be merciful,' Hussain yelled.

Then two policemen came and the man was escorted away. The shopkeepers went back to their shops in triumph. Hussain walked towards Sayeed, shaking his head sadly and gesturing with his hands his uselessness in trying to help the man.

'Too many foreigners,' one shopkeeper shouted.

'Without them we would not have much business here,' another shouted back, and started laughing.

Latifa was frightened. She was holding Leila's hand tightly.

'Let us go home quickly,' she said.

'Don't worry, Latifa. These things happen in the city quite often,' Sayeed said.

'They nearly assaulted Hussain,' she said, turning towards Sayeed.

'He should not have gone there. It was none of his business. It is better to walk away from those things,' Sayeed said.

'I cannot ignore injustice. I must be able to sleep,' Hussain said with a smile.

'I am sure you can sleep well. But if you go to jail, then you will not be able to sleep,' Sayeed said.

They started walking along the lanes, towards the car park.

'I would like to come and see the gold souk next time,' Latifa said.

'Do you want to go there now?' Hussain asked.

'No, Leila is tired now. It's getting late as well. We will come again soon,' Latifa said.

Chapter 21

The following day Sayeed went back to work. All his friends were happy that he was married. He told everyone about the wedding ceremony, and he felt as if he were the most important person in the world.

But as the weeks went by, Latifa still did not get used to life in the shanty town. Her main worry was Leila, who played with children who were not washed by their parents. She was afraid that Leila might catch some disease from them.

The woman who lived next to Sayeed's hut was about fifty, and her husband was a labourer who worked in the city. She had a herd of goats which she took to the desert every morning. At first she was friendly with Latifa, but later she stopped talking to her, and started passing acerbic remarks whenever she saw her. Latifa could not understand the reason for this. She could not remember doing anything antagonistic to her. The woman's children were grown up and had left home. They came only rarely to see her. She managed to stir up detestation among the other women towards Latifa.

This was very depressing for Latifa. She went to see the *mutawah*'s wife who spoke to the other woman, but she still refused to be friendly. Perhaps it was because she was a newcomer, the *mutawah*'s wife said. She might be friendlier to her after a while.

Latifa stayed inside the hut most of the time. Leila played outside. Sometimes the other children threw sand at her, and she came running inside crying, with sand in her eyes.

Soon the child began to want to go home. Latifa was getting frightened to go outside. Sayeed told her to be patient.

'They will be all right later. This is one of their ways of getting rid of people from this area, because it is getting very crowded,' Sayeed said.

'Some of them laugh at me, and our next-door neighbour is wicked,' Latifa said.

'Just ignore them. They will get fed up, then they will stop,' Sayeed said.

'I don't want to fight with them. I think some of them are jealous. Most of them are very poor. They do not have enough money to dress or eat,' Latifa said.

'Yes. This may be the reason. Also you are much younger than most of them. Perhaps they envy you.' Sayeed smiled.

'I don't know how you can smile. Some of these women have become very hostile, and it is only the mutawah's family that I can trust. I don't know most of the other women, but this creature has turned all of them against me,' Latifa said.

'It's simple. Invite some of them to have tea, and try to get friendly with them,' Sayeed suggested.

'I cannot imagine the thing from next door becoming friendly. She spits whenever she sees me. I cannot understand why, and some of the children are very foul to Leila. She has a little friend, a girl who comes here early in the morning, and plays with her, but the others, especially the older ones, are very rough,' Latifa said. 'I want to go back to the village,' she added quietly.

'What? How can you do that!'

'I do not think we can live here. It has been nearly four weeks now, and I am fed up. Just look outside: dirt and filth, little huts made up of old pieces of wooden boxes. Look at our hut, not much better either. The people are mean, the smell is bad. That is not so noticeable now. Perhaps my nose is getting used to it. Not enough water to have a proper wash or shower. I cannot see how I can stay here.'

'You will get used to it.'

'I won't, and I don't think the child will either.'

'The child seems to be happy.'

'That's what you think! She misses her grandparents, and cries a lot. You are at work most of the time, you don't see that. Look outside, it's all desert. No green plants. Back at the village, all around us are trees, green plants, and plenty of water too. No problem with neighbours. People are clean. Why do we have to suffer? Why don't we all go back to the village, then we could farm? Hard work, yes. Little money as well. But we could be happy back at the village.'

'My work is at the hospital. They pay much more money than I could earn by farming. Fruit and vegetables are cheap because they import a great deal from other countries. It's good for the consumer, but not very good for the farmer. There is some money in animal farming, but even that will be finished soon, because of cheap imported animals, and the big factory farming places they have started.'

'You seem to know a great deal about farming,'

'I cannot read, but I listen to people. There are quite a few people at the hospital doing similar jobs to mine. They have been farmers too. Also remember that I have to pay back a lot of money to the hospital. That is another reason to stay. It will take about two years to pay off that loan. So, please, do not think of other things. Try to settle down.'

'I can't. If you don't take me home, I am going to go back somehow. I will walk away to the desert with my child,' Latifa said, and got up and went outside.

Sayeed was angry. He could not make her understand the serious situation that he was in. The wedding had been very costly, and it would take years to recover financially, and now she wanted to go back home. He hoped she might forget what she had said, and probably would feel settled in time.

He went to work in the hospital as usual in the mornings, and came back late, then took the family to the city sometimes. After a few days, Latifa stopped doing any work, or any cooking. The child got used to going out and playing, and Latifa stopped worrying about her, how she looked, or whether she was clean or not. The child liked this. She was free to do whatever she wished. Latifa slept for long periods during the day. At night, Sayeed slept in his room, on his own.

When Sayeed came home he washed and cleaned the child, and went to the shop, bought some food, cooked it. Sometimes he bought some cooked food from the city.

Latifa sat in a corner quietly and did not say anything. She stared at her feet stretched out in front of her, and now and then gave a deep sigh. She did not comb her hair or change her clothes for days. In the beginning, Sayeed thought she was a little sad, but would shake it off and be back to normal soon, but after two weeks she was getting worse. Sayeed thought he should take her to the hospital, but when he suggested this to her, she refused. She stopped crying too. Sayeed discussed it with the *mutawah*, who said she should be taken back to her village immediately. He blamed Sayeed for not coming to see him earlier, and for not taking her to see her parents sooner.

'She will be all right. She misses her family. Do not bring her back too soon,' the *mutawah* said.

'When she gets better, and if she wants to come back, then she can. If not, I am going to let her stay in the village,' Sayeed said.

'Oh, no. She must come back. She is your wife. You can't live without her, and you mustn't. Women get used to anything. They are much tougher than men. By the way, has she been sick in the morning?' the *mutawah* asked.

'No,' Sayeed said.

Sayeed told Abdul Mubarak what was happening to Latifa. When he was ready to take her to the village, Abdul came in his car and took them there.

Latifa's parents were shocked to see the state she was in. It was about six weeks since she had married. They all cried, except Latifa. She stared at her parents as if she were looking at strangers. The child hugged her grandfather, and told him how much she had missed him.

Akila and Halima were sorry to see Latifa unwell. Mustafa understood.

'I told you, it is a very hard life there for a woman,' he said to Sayeed.

The following day, Sayeed went back to the city with Abdul.

Latifa slept in her old room most of the time, and after a few days she began to recover. It had been like a nightmare. She did not want to discuss anything with her parents. It was their fault, she thought. Slowly, she began to get back to normal, and was very glad that she had come back. She began to cry, holding on to her parents, and they reassured her that they would look after her.

All her hopes for a better life were just a dream which never came true. Instead, she had been through unexpected horrors. She began to recall life back in the shanty town but she did not remember much of the last two weeks there. Sometimes she thought it was her fault. She had never gone to the neighbours' huts when they had invited her, and she had never invited any of them to her hut. The only contact that she had was with the *mutawah*'s family. Even they had stopped visiting her because she did not visit them.

Sayeed came several times during the few weeks that she was back. He brought presents for her and the child, and was trying to persuade her to go back with him to the city. But she refused. Then her parents also started urging her to go back with Sayeed. They suggested that she should take some goats with her and build a herd. That would keep her busy, her father said. 'The important thing is – give me a grandson,' the old man whispered in Sayeed's ear. Sayeed smiled and looked away.

After several weeks back at the village, Latifa at last

decided to go back to the city. She felt determined to face the hard life. And she also felt strong enough to face the women back at the shanty town.

Chapter 22

Latifa's father gave her a few goats. Three nanny goats, one with a month-old kid, and two billy goats. Leila was pleased to hear that the kid was coming with them. He also arranged a truck and a driver to transport the goats to the city. Sayeed had come to collect his family, and Mustafa had been pestered by his women to take them to the city when Latifa went back. They wanted to go and see the women who were bothering Latifa, and they managed to get one of their friends to stay at home with their children while they were away.

Both trucks left at the same time. Sayeed with Akila, and Halima in Mustafa's truck. Latifa, her child and parents in the truck with the goats. Mustafa's truck went ahead. It was a long journey. Latifa was apprehensive about her parents seeing their small hut, but they had insisted on it, and she could not persuade them to change their minds. Akila and Halima were angry. They wanted to speak to the women, and to see the city that had made Latifa ill.

On the way, they left the main road and stopped in a quiet place in the desert, near some sand dunes, and had a meal which they had brought from home. They sat on mats on the sand, talking about the wedding and some of the amusing things that had happened then.

When they came to the shanty town, it was towards the end of the afternoon. The sun was still orange, and the air was hot. Latifa's parents and Halima and Akila had all been told beforehand by Latifa about the type of hut and the area they lived in, to avoid any shock when they arrived.

What Akila commented on was the smell. As she entered the town she pinched her nostrils, and started breathing through her mouth.

'You will not smell anything soon,' Mustafa said.

'Why is that?' Akila asked, without taking her fingers off her nostrils.

'You will get used to it,' he laughed.

'I hope it does not stick to my clothes,' Akila said, taking her fingers off her nostrils.

When the truck stopped in front of their hut, some of Sayeed's friends came out of their huts to greet them. The next-door neighbour's wife came out too, and started shouting. She was more annoyed when she saw that they had brought goats as well.

'I curse you all to perish soon. You can take your infectious goats back,' she said in a very loud voice, throwing her hands up in the air.

Akila and Halima got out of the truck quickly, and both started shouting at the woman.

'You old hag, we curse you a thousand times over,' Halima said.

'These goats are going to stay here, and you can stay with them in the pen we are going to build,' Akila said.

'You are not going to build any animal pens around here. There is no room. Everyone in the country wants to come and live in this area because it is good here,' the woman said.

'This is not your land. It belongs to the government, and we will get the police to sort you out,' Akila said.

'Go! Go! Go to the police,' the woman shouted at the top of her voice.

Some women were watching, but no one joined the woman.

'Aren't you going to say anything? You stupid lot! You had so much to say about this princess, and we thought she had left here for good, but now she is back again, with a few goats and two donkeys,' the woman said, pointing to Akila and Halima.

'We are not donkeys. You are the donkey,' Halima said, and with a clenched fist, she started to walk towards the woman. 'I am going to break your teeth, and send them down your camel's belly,' she said.

The woman got frightened, and withdrew slowly into her hut, still shouting. All the spectators started to laugh. The woman's voice could be heard coming from her hut, still cursing, and she had started to throw cooking pots everywhere. Some women who had been unfriendly to Latifa in the past came and greeted her, and said how glad they were to see her back.

'That woman is mad,' one of the younger women said to Latifa.

Halima and Akila were pleased that they had frightened the woman.

'I don't think you will have any more problems with her,' Halima said.

'After you have gone, she might start again,' Latifa said.

'No, she will not, we will see to that,' one of the women said.

'If she does, tell her that you will call me,' Halima said with a laugh.

Latifa's parents were silent. But they were pleased to hear the other neighbours were on Latifa's side. Mustafa and Sayeed, their arms folded, were leaning against the front of the truck, laughing. The woman's cursing was still to be heard from the hut. The crowd started to disperse, and the visitors entered Sayeed's house.

They had some tea, and Mustafa and Sayeed built a short, round fence at the back of the hut for the goats, and caged them there.

The men explored the area, while the women did the cooking. They ate their evening meal with fresh peta bread Sayeed had bought at the local shop, and went to sleep. Mustafa and the other driver slept in their trucks, and the rest slept inside the hut.

The following day Sayeed had to go to work, and the others went to the city. First they went to the gold *souk*. Akila and Halima bought gold bangles for themselves, and Latifa bought two gold chains, one for herself, and the other for the child. Afterwards they went to the cloth *souk* and Halima and Akila bought cloth for their children.

'It's better to shop in the evening. It's too hot at this time of the day,' Mustafa said.

'Not many shops are open during the day either,' Latifa said.

'We must leave today. The children are at home,' Halima said.

'I think we ought to wait until Sayeed comes home,' Akila said.

'He doesn't come home till late. You have a long way to go,' Latifa said.

They went back to the hut. The neighbour was attending to her goats. When she saw that they had come back, she looked the other way, but did not say anything.

The visitors ate some lunch. Early in the afternoon they decided to start their return journey.

'Please tell Sayeed we could not wait for him,' Halima said.

'He was hoping you would stay, but you have a long way to go,' Latifa said.

Latifa's parents were very sad to leave Leila and Latifa behind.

'We are old, and we do not think that we can do this journey very often. So you must come and see us, Latifa,' her father said.

'I will try, father,' Latifa said.

'You be brave, now. Don't let them get you down,' Halima said.

All the women hugged and kissed Latifa and the child, while Mustafa looked on thoughtfully.

'Give them plenty of water,' Latifa's father said, pointing towards the goats.

'Don't worry, I will look after them,' Latifa said.

'Now you don't have to buy animals for the Haaj ceremony,' Mustafa said.

Latifa looked at the child but fortunately she did not seem to understand what Mustafa implied.

It was very hot in the early afternoon. The desert had become like a furnace. They all got into the trucks. Mustafa and the other driver started to drive slowly with the air-conditioners on and the windows shut. Latifa and the child stood outside the hut, waving, and watched the trucks go on the dust track, and then on to the tarred road, until they disappeared. The whole of the shanty area was deserted. In the midday heat it was impossible for anyone to stay outside. Latifa went inside the hut with her child. She felt very lonely, but she was surprised that the child did not cry this time. She sat near the desert cooler, and her child sat on her lap and started to suck her thumb. She took a handful of sunflower seeds from a dish on the floor, and started eating them, a few at a time, spitting out the shells towards the corner.

Latifa felt as if a new life was beginning. She was brave now, and was determined to fight back and survive. She no longer felt helpless.

It was cool inside. Everywhere was quiet, except for the blowing that came from the desert cooler. She fell asleep.

When she woke up, it was late in the afternoon. The goats in the pen outside were restless. Latifa got up and went outside to check on them. They had knocked over the bucket of water, and their food was almost finished. She filled up the water container, and gave them some feed which was stored in a sack just outside the hut. The goats all tried to put their heads in the bucket at the same time. She did not want to let them out of the pen yet, in case they wandered away.

Sayeed came back earlier than usual and was very sorry to learn that everyone had gone. He had brought some grass for the animals. Leila was happy, because he had brought her some sweets. Sayeed had also bought some lamb for the guests.

'Do you want to cook this today, or shall I buy some cooked chicken from the shop?' Sayeed asked.

'Don't worry. It doesn't take long to cook this. We will have a good meal tonight,' Latifa said.

'I like the way you cooked lamb when you first came here,' Sayeed said.

'How did I do that? I cannot remember,' Latifa said.

'You cut it into small pieces, fried it a little with some spices, then added chopped tomatoes, lots of them, and a few chopped green chilli peppers, and some garlic . . .' Sayeed continued.

'Oh, yes. Yes, if that's how you like it, I will cook it that way,' Latifa said.

'We need some bread, I will go to the shop later on and bring some freshly baked bread,' Sayeed said.

'Please bring some eggs as well. Leila does not like meat very much. Perhaps I could make her an omelette,' Latifa said.

'You look happy!' Sayeed said.

'Well, I am trying to be,' Latifa said.

Chapter 23

Hussain Hasmi brought a truckload of wood which he had collected from the desert, and some from a pile thrown away on a building site. Sayeed had asked him to bring it so that they could build an animal shed for the goats.

That evening, Sayeed and Hussain Hasmi started work on it. They built a small shed, between the hut and the toilet. They had to dig deep to bury the four poles at each corner for the shed, because the top sand was soft, and then they nailed pieces of planks to the poles. The flat roof was covered with hardboard pieces, and some corrugated iron. Then they covered it with a plastic sheet, and placed some heavy pieces of wood on top to hold it down. It was not very high, they had to bend down slightly to go in. A small door was fixed facing their hut. It was almost dark by the time they had finished.

Latifa made several glasses of tea, and they drank them while they worked. Leila was watching them, she wanted to nail the planks with the hammer. Sayeed refused at first, but had to give in and let her try, but soon she got fed up, and started feeding the little kid with handfuls of grass.

After the construction of the animal house, Sayeed

and Hussain came in, and ate the camel meat that Latifa had cooked for supper. Hussain commented on its taste, and Latifa who was eating with the child in the other room heard him. Sayeed was glad that he had someone to help him. After the meal, Hussain said that he was going to the city. Sayeed was tired, and wanted to stay at home.

The following day, Sayeed was off work. He had suggested to Latifa that they should take the goats to the desert, to find places where they could be grazed. Leila was delighted with the idea, and they all had their breakfast early, and Sayeed opened the door of the animal shed, and led the goats with a stick towards the desert.

Sayeed walked behind the goats with a stick in his hand, and Latifa and Leila walked behind him. They walked on the main track towards the middle of the shanty town, then turned on to a small track leading to the desert.

'We must get back before it gets too hot,' Sayeed said.

'It's already hot. We have got only two cans of Pepsi with us,' Latifa said.

They headed for the tall rocky area towards the east, following the animal tracks which were easier to walk on because they had been worn smooth and were clear of sharp-edged rocks. Now and then the goats would find small thorny bushes with a few small green leaves, and they would gently run their tongues over the thorns, pulling the leaves out efficiently, and eating them, kneeling on their front legs.

Latifa and Leila were walking slowly, and they were getting left behind.

'We mustn't go very far,' Sayeed said.

'There are plenty of things for them to eat here. Why don't we stay here,' Latifa said, putting both her hands on her hips and stretching.

'I want to go up that hill,' Leila said.

'Some other time. It's a bit far, and my legs are killing me,' Latifa said.

'We haven't walked that far, but if you are tired, we will sit down here and rest for a while. The animals can feed on the shrubs here,' Sayeed said.

Latifa sat on a piece of rock.

'That rock in the distance is quite tall. Perhaps we should go there one day,' Latifa said.

'You cannot see it from here, but before you go to the rock, there is a big drop to the valley below. When it rains, it becomes like a big river. It is difficult to get down there, the climb down is dangerous,' Sayeed said.

'Can't you go around it?' Latifa asked.

'Yes, you can. But to do that you have to walk a long way, then climb down to the flat desert, then climb up again to the rock,' Sayeed said.

'I wouldn't mind that. I would like to go there one day,' Latifa said.

'Your legs ache already! How could you walk that far?'

'I will try. You will be surprised what I can do,' Latifa laughed.

They opened the Pepsi cans, and the froth spilled out. Leila had a can to herself, and Latifa and Sayeed shared one.

'I think we had better go back now,' Latifa said, getting up.

'Perhaps you could bring the goats by yourself next time,' Sayeed said to Latifa.

'I would be worried.'

'No, you will be all right. Our nasty neighbour brings her goats here. Look out there! Your friend is there now with her goats,' Sayeed said, pointing to their hostile neighbour with her goats in the distance.

'I suppose I will have to do that soon. You go to work every day, and you don't have much time for these animals. Buying food for them is expensive,' Latifa said.

'If we had a herd, we could earn a lot of money,' Sayeed said.

'Yes, but they would need a lot of looking after, I don't think I could do it on my own,' Latifa said.

'One thing you must remember is not to let them wander away towards the valley,' Sayeed said.

'I am used to looking after animals. I know how to keep them under control,' Latifa said.

Sayeed hit the goats with his stick, and started chasing them towards the shanty town. The animals were reluctant to leave their grazing but one goat took the lead, and started to walk towards the town, and the rest followed. The goat kid started to stray. Leila began chasing it, and it went in between the rest of the goats, and started walking with them. They took the same route back, and walked through the shanty town. One of their neighbours was outside hanging her clothes on a line. She greeted Latifa, and asked her to come and visit. Latifa agreed to visit her later that day.

They drove the goats into the animal house, locked them in, went inside their hut, turned the desert cooler on, and sat near it.

'I will take you to the city today,' Sayeed said.

'I would like that, even if we don't buy anything, it is nice to walk around that area,' Latifa said.

'This time we will walk up to the main road and take a taxi,' Sayeed said.

'If you want, but won't that be expensive?' Latifa asked.

'No, not very, I can haggle with them,' Sayeed said.

'I still miss my village, but not so much now,' Latifa said.

'That is good. The city is not bad once you get used to it. Just think, there are thousands of people like us living here,' Sayeed said.

'I hope you will find a good house for us soon,' Latifa said.

'As soon as we get more money. At the moment this house does not cost me anything. If I were to rent a house or a flat, I would have to pay a lot of money. So let us be patient,' Sayeed said.

That afternoon Sayeed and his family went to visit the neighbour who had called to them earlier that day. Her daughter, Shamim, and Leila had become friends, and they played together, outside on the sand, and visited each other's huts. Shamim's mother Huda was about the same age as Latifa.

Latifa was glad that she now had a friend whom she could trust in the neighbourhood. Huda asked her to visit them again. Her husband, who worked as a porter at the nearby National Guard Primary Health Care Unit, had been a friend of Sayeed for some time.

Chapter 24

The following morning, Latifa woke up late, after Sayeed had gone to work. It was bright, and it was beginning to get hot. Leila was sleeping on the mattress next to her. Suddenly Latifa noticed how quiet it was. She got up, opened the back door, and walked towards the animal house. The door of the shed was open, and all the goats were gone. She went around the shed, and around the hut quickly, but the goats were not to be seen anywhere. Then she noticed some tracks heading towards the desert.

She ran inside. Leila was sitting on the floor, holding on to her doll. Latifa told her to put her slippers on quickly, because she was going to Huda's hut to play. The child was happy, and she got ready. Latifa put a pair of slippers on, locked the doors, and walked quickly towards Huda's hut.

Huda was glad to keep Leila in her hut, but she wanted to go with Latifa to find the goats. Latifa said that she would not trouble her, and that the goats could not be far away. So she left the child with Huda, rushed towards the animal house, and started following the tracks. It was not easy to distinguish their tracks because there were so many others, but further on the tracks were clear, and there was no doubt that they were the ones made by her goats. They were leaving the shanty town, towards the desert, but the goats were still not to be seen. She followed the tracks with quickening strides. There was no one around the huts in the shanty area, it was all quiet. The sand was soft, and the tracks were clearly visible.

She walked further and further, away from the shanty town, towards the desert. She could see the tall rock, far away in the desert. Behind her, the huts in the shanty town were beginning to disappear. She came to the end of the soft sand, and started to walk on the rugged rocky area. No tracks from her goats could be distinguished now, only the usual ones of the animals which used that route daily.

It was very hot. She had not even drunk a glass of water before she had left home. She was thirsty, and she was hungry too. The heat was intense and she was sweating but she did not want to slow down her stride in case the animals got further and further away.

The houses looked very small now, and the rock was beginning to seem bigger. She could see the valley which Sayeed had mentioned the day before.

This was the first time that she had come this far since she had been living here. She was getting worried and quite frightened. But she did not want to go back without the goats.

So many thoughts started to flash through her mind, and she was thirsty and hungry. Since she had come back from her village, she had not enjoyed a meal yet. There were not enough cooking facilities, and Sayeed could not afford to buy good meat and other good food. For the first few weeks, after she was brought from the village after the marriage, it was unbearable. They ate like paupers, and when she started to think about the food that her mother cooked, and the food that they had prepared when her first husband was alive, she felt sad. She also felt sad when she remembered the luscious green trees back home in the village. Here it was all shanty huts and rugged desert. She also remembered the abuse and insults that she had encountered from her neighbours. They had stopped now, but it was difficult to forget. The constant bad smell in the shanty town of unwashed bodies, litter and garbage, human and animal excrement, was something that she was getting used to. When she did not think about it, she did not smell anything at all. Now she was getting tired, her feet were aching, and the sun's glare was filtering through her veil.

She could no longer see the huts. All around her was the desert. It was empty. She could not even see her wicked neighbour who usually brought her animals to the desert. The tall rock was closer now. The valley was in front of her, and she stood at the edge of it. The zigzagged valley continued to the west, towards the flat, red sandy desert, in the direction in which she was walking. The tall rock was on the other side of the valley. She looked down, towards the bottom of the valley, and could see the goats down there, among the thorny bushes, feeding on the scanty leaves.

She was tired, and very frightened at being alone. It was a long climb down to the bottom of the valley. She sat down, and slowly started to slide. Then one of her slippers came off, and rolled away down the hill, hitting the rocks. It was thrown into the air, then it completely vanished over some thorny bushes below.

She was frightened that she might fall down too. For a moment she could not move. She thought it would be unwise either to look down towards the bottom of the valley, or look up. So she looked at her feet, and slowly started to slide down, holding on to the rocks, and to the bushes on the slope. It was difficult without the slipper on her right foot.

The goats saw Latifa, and started bleating, but carried on eating the leaves. She was holding on to the bushes, her hands and feet covered with dust which had become mixed with her sweat, turning it to mud. Slowly, she reached the bottom of the valley and looked up. She could see how tall the slope was, and she did not know how she could go back with the goats. It might be better if she went along the valley with them, towards the flat, red sandy area, then around the tall rock, towards the shanty town. She picked a piece of stick and started hitting the goats. She was very angry. The goats started to run, then they began to climb towards the tall rock. Then she realised the mistake that she had made, and started to walk towards them, with the staff hidden behind her.

She heard the sound of a vehicle, far away in the desert. She felt relieved. But then she could not hear anything. She thought she was imagining it. It was all quiet again.

The thirst was unbearable, and she felt dizzy. She sat on a rock, under a bush, and licked off some sweat on her arms. The salty, dust-covered hand was hot, and the taste of salt and dust made her nauseous.

Her lips were dry. She was puffing, and her tongue was getting dry too. She lay there, watching the goats climb up the valley, towards the tall rock. They were feeding on the leaves of the short bushes as they climbed.

She got up, and felt as if the valley were spinning

around her. She quickly grabbed a branch of a thorny bush to stop herself from falling. At the same time, her foot without the slipper hit the sharp edge of a rock, and a gaping cut appeared just below her ankle, and started to bleed profusely. The thorns in the bush pierced the flesh in her hand. She was in great pain and cried out loud.

She thought she should never have gone there on her own. She should have taken Huda's offer of help. There was no one around. They would not be able to find her, she thought. She started calling for help, but her mouth was dry. Words did not come. Her hands were bleeding, and her foot was bleeding badly, too. She sat up again, felt around her ankle, and started to sob. The blood was coming fast, so she took off her veil and tied it around her ankle. It was bleeding, but not so badly now. She knew that she had to make an effort to reach the top. Then she heard the sound of a vehicle again, but she was not sure now whether it was real.

She started climbing towards the tall rock. The goats were still. They stopped feeding, and looked down towards Latifa. She was crawling up slowly, dragging her injured foot, sobbing, and wiping her tears and sweat on the sleeves of her *abaya*. She remembered Leila, and started to sob louder.

The only way now was to go up towards the goats, and drive them down, towards the bottom of the valley, and then drive them quickly around the tall rock, towards the shanty town. So she started climbing up, hands stretched above her, holding on to rocks that were not loose, pushing herself up with her good foot, and dragging the injured one.

Suddenly she felt some small stones falling down

towards her, and she looked up. She could see the goats were disturbed. They were looking towards the right side of the rock above them. Latifa looked towards it, where she saw the silhouetted figure of someone standing there. She could not distinguish whether it was a man or a woman. She called for help, but the voice came out as a whisper. She gathered all her strength and yelled for help. The sound was coarse and loud.

'I am coming down. You wait there,' a man's voice said.

'Who is that?'

'Hussain Hasmi. Do you need help?'

'Yes, yes. Please. I cannot move any more. Please help,' Latifa called, and started sobbing.

'Do not move, wait there. I am coming down,' Hussain said.

'Please hurry,' Latifa begged, staying motionless, with stretched hands holding on to the rocks above her, and supporting herself by pushing herself up with her good leg.

Hussain Hasmi came down quickly, and grabbed one of her hands. She looked up, and looked at his face. He was sitting down and holding on to her hand, and she felt safe.

'You have got blood on your hand. Are you hurt?' he asked.

'I pricked myself with some thorns. It hurts very badly,' she said.

'Now you push yourself up, slowly, and I will take you up there. There is a shady spot up there.'

'My foot is also injured. It is still bleeding,' she sobbed.

'All right, I will take you up there. Then you can rest

in the shade. My truck is on the other side, I will take you home soon,' Hussain reassured her.

'I am glad you came. We must catch the goats first,' she said.

'Never mind the goats now. I will come back for them,' Hussain said.

'I am very thirsty, I have never felt so thirsty in my life,' Latifa said, almost in a whisper.

'All right, just a bit more, we are almost there. There is a shady cave, I will take you there,' Hussain said, pointing to the cave which was almost halfway up the rock.

The last few metres to the cave were not so steep, so Latifa stood up, walked slowly, limping, holding on to Hussain's hand.

He brought her into the shade, and sat her down on the ground, against a smooth rock which was near the entrance to the cave.

'I have never seen your face before,' Hussain said, looking at Latifa's damp face. 'You are very beautiful.'

She put her head back slowly, and rested it against the rock, and her hands flopped lifelessly on the ground.

'Water, water. I am very thirsty, and my leg aches, my body aches, and I think I am going to die,' she said, stretching her legs in front of her.

'No, no, Latifa, you are going to be all right. Please wait,' he said, and he sat near her. 'Your ankle is still bleeding. Let me have a look,' he said, and he took off the veil which she had tied around it. The wound was open, and Latifa started crying loudly. He tied it back again, as gently as possible, and looked at his hands. They were covered with blood. He slowly wiped the blood off his fingers on her calf, raised her dress gently, and kissed her leg. She withdrew the leg quickly, and looked at his face. Sweat was pouring down his cheeks. His eyes were fixed on her, and his lips were trembling. She wanted to scream, resist, run away. He started lifting up her dress slowly, and his bloodstained fingers left bloody lines up her leg over her knee, and up her thigh. She could not push him away, she did not push him away. No feeling of thirst any more, and her mouth was no longer dry. Her injured hand and her wounded leg were no longer painful. She could smell his after-shave. She could smell his sweat. She could feel his clean-shaven face. She felt no fear of anyone, and she felt as if she were the happiest person on earth at that moment. She screamed, and she laughed, and her voice came out unhindered.

Hussain got up. She tried to grab him, and pull him down, but he got up fast. She lay there, with her dress still not pushed down. Her wounded ankle and her injured hand were painful again. Her thirst came back, and she was in agony. Hussain was standing with his back to her. She could see the red desert below, and far away in the distance, the Mirage.

She saw heads popping around the corner of the cave. Several people stood up. Hussain saw them at the same time. He ran past them, as fast as he could. They tried to catch him, but he pushed several of them. He ran fast, got into his truck, and drove away at a very high speed.

Latifa pushed her dress down, and got up quickly.

'You dirty whore, you said you were coming to look for your goats,' Huda yelled. She picked up some stones and threw them at Latifa. One stone struck Latifa's head, she screamed, and her head started to bleed.

The *mutawah* came running with his stick, and started

to cane her non-stop. She was screaming as loud as she could, begging for mercy, but all the others, about ten of their neighbours, men and women, were shouting at her, throwing stones at her, and some women were kicking her. She started to run. They were chasing her. The *mutawah* caned her while she ran, and the others showered her with stones. She was covering her head with both hands, but the stones were hitting her body all over. Latifa wailed, screamed, and fell down. The women kicked her, on her body, on her face. Blood was coming out of the corner of her mouth, and from her open mouth with blood-covered teeth came a groaning noise.

Then she stood up very quickly, and started to run towards the brow of the valley, near the tall rock.

'This was all planned, this whore and that animal,' Huda said, throwing stones at Latifa. She tried to run as fast as she could, but it was not enough. She flopped down, and the women started again to kick her body all over. She lay there, still conscious, bleeding from her face, head, hands, and all over. But she did not feel pain any more. With her mouth slightly open, and her white teeth covered with clots of blood, she stayed motionless.

They carried her, and threw her on to the back of a truck. They all got in, and one of them started to drive the truck back to the shanty town.

'I have been watching them for some time,' the *mutawah* said.

'I did not know any of this. I thought you were coming to help me find her,' Huda said.

'I saw him driving towards the rock; then you came and told me that she had gone as well. I got suspicious,' the *mutawah* said.

'Dirty animals, both of them,' Huda said, and she spat

at Latifa who was lying on the floor of the truck. Huda was sitting in a corner, and in the other sat the *mutawah* with some of the neighbours.

'I brought all these good people as witnesses,' the *mutawah* said with a smile.

Latifa could hear the conversation, but she could not move a muscle. She felt as if she was completely paralysed. She was still bleeding, her hair was wet with blood, and flies started hovering over her. The truck was travelling fast, and her body was bouncing up and down. The others were trying to hold on to the sides of the truck, and now and then someone cursed, and spat on her.

Latifa was taken to the shanty town, and was pulled off the truck, and dumped outside her hut.

The *mutawah* summoned the religious police, and they came in a black van, loaded her in, and took her to jail.

Chapter 25

When Sayeed came home, he found the hut in darkness, the doors locked, and no answer when he knocked on the door. He called for Latifa and Leila. He went to Huda's hut. Leila was playing with Huda's daughter.

'Where is your mother?' Sayeed asked Leila.

'She went looking for the goats, a long time ago, and is not back yet. I want to go home, Uncle Sayeed,' she said.

Huda was quiet. She stood in the corner of her sitting-room, her face veiled, and her arms folded.

'Where is Latifa?' Sayeed asked Huda.

'I don't know. Go and ask the mutawah,' she said.

'Mutawah! Why the mutawah? Where is she?' Sayeed cried.

'Go and see him. He will tell you all about her,' Huda said in a firm voice.

'All right, Huda, I am going. I am sorry you had to look after Leila. I will take her now,' Sayeed said.

'You can leave her here. I am just going to give them something to eat,' Huda offered.

'All right, I will be back soon,' Sayeed said, and he left and walked towards the *mutawah*'s hut. On the way there, he saw several of his friends, but when they saw Sayeed coming they slowly walked away in another direction. Sayeed was puzzled. He walked fast.

'Where is my wife, mutawah?'

'In jail.'

'What? What has she done?' Sayeed said in amazement.

'I warned you about Hussain Hasmi several times, and we caught both of them in the desert. He ran away, she is in the jail now.'

'Oh please, what happened? Poor woman. This is not true. It is not possible.' Sayeed started crying. He crouched down on the floor, and kept slapping his head with both hands and wailing loudly.

The *mutawah* sat on the sitting-room carpet, leaning against the cushion and continuing to sip his cardamom coffee.

'We had a lot of witnesses. I am afraid she was a bit injured,' the *mutawah* said.

'What have you done to her? Poor woman! It's all my fault. I brought her to this hell,' Sayeed said, and he got up, and walked fast towards Huda's hut.

Leila was eating. He held her hand, lifted her up, hugged her, and started kissing her.

'Why are you crying, Uncle Sayeed?' Leila asked.

'No, I am not crying,' he said, wiping his eyes.

Huda stood motionless.

'Let us go home now, Leila,' Sayeed said.

He went home, kicked the door down, and got some of Leila's clothes, and some of his, put them in several bags, and collected all the money and the valuables that he had in the hut, and started walking towards the main road with Leila in one hand, and the bags in the other.

He took a taxi and went to the hospital, and told Hameed what had happened. Someone telephoned Abdul Mubarak, and he came quickly. Sayeed left the child with Hameed, and went with Abdul Mubarak to find the jail where they had taken Latifa.

They drove to several women's jails and inquired, but none of them had her. They drove around the city, and it was after midnight when they managed to find the prison where Latifa was being kept. The guard stood at his post, behind the locked gates, with his machine gun, and told them to come back the following day.

They went back to the hospital. Abdul Mubarak said his sister would look after Leila, so he took her with him. Sayeed slept in the laboratory.

Sayeed and Abdul went back to the jail the following morning. There was a clerk near the entrance. He checked the name, and gave the date of Latifa's court hearing. It was in three days' time. Sayeed started begging to be allowed to see Latifa. The guard laughed, and told him to go away, otherwise he was going to lock him up. Sayeed told them to lock him up too, but Abdul Mubarak quickly took him away, and drove him back to the hospital.

Sayeed felt helpless. Abdul Mubarak volunteered to drive Sayeed back to the village, to tell Latifa's family about her. Sayeed refused, and said he would never go back home.

The court hearing was brief. There were enough witnesses to commit Latifa for adultery. They had caught Hussain Hasmi too.

Latifa was to be put to death by stoning. It was to be carried out the following Friday after the midday prayers.

They sentenced Hussain Hasmi to death by beheading. That was to be carried out the same day.

Sayeed started crying loudly.

'Please forgive them,' he cried.

The guards came and dragged him outside. He started to struggle with them. They pushed him to the ground. He lay there wailing loudly and slapping the Earth with both hands.